THE MYSTERY
OF THE
PERIODIC TABLE

The Mystery
of the
Periodic Table

Benjamin D. Wiker

Chapter heading illustrations
by Jeanne Bendick
Technical drawings by Theodore Schluenderfritz

Bethlehem Books • Ignatius Press
Bathgate, N.D.   San Francisco

Text © 2003 Benjamin D. Wiker
Chapter illustrations © 2003 Jeanne Bendick
Technical drawings © 2003 Theodore Schluenderfritz

Cover design by Davin Carlson

First printing, May 2003

ISBN: 1-883937-71-X
Library of Congress catalog number: 2003102229

Bethlehem Books • Ignatius Press
10194 Garfield St. South
Bathgate, ND 58216
www.bethlehembooks.com
1-800-757-6831

Printed in the United States on acid-free paper

Contents

Acknowledgments

I would like to thank editors Peter Sharpe and especially Lydia Reynolds at Bethlehem Books for their kind and patient guidance, and Mike Keas and Dan Barrett for reading over the manuscript and providing many very helpful suggestions. (Of course, any errors are my own.) I'd also like to thank Thomas Aquinas College for its kind assistance in providing appropriate historical materials (and also inspiring editor Peter Sharpe for this project with its wonderful second year chemistry course.) Finally, in gratitude to my loving wife, Teresa, and seven children, especially my three oldest, Jacob, Anna, and Faith, who read the manuscript and helped me make it accessible to younger readers.

Periodic Table of the Elements

1A	2A	3B	4B	5B	6B	7B	8B	8B	8B	1B	2B	3A	4A	5A	6A	7A	8A
1 H 1.008																	2 He 4.003
3 Li 6.941	4 Be 9.012											5 B 10.81	6 C 12.01	7 N 14.01	8 O 16.00	9 F 19.00	10 Ne 20.18
11 Na 22.99	12 Mg 24.31											13 Al 26.98	14 Si 28.09	15 P 30.97	16 S 32.06	17 Cl 35.45	18 Ar 39.95
19 K 39.10	20 Ca 40.08	21 Sc 44.96	22 Ti 47.90	23 V 50.94	24 Cr 52.00	25 Mn 54.94	26 Fe 55.85	27 Co 58.93	28 Ni 58.70	29 Cu 63.55	30 Zn 65.38	31 Ga 69.72	32 Ge 72.59	33 As 74.92	34 Se 78.96	35 Br 79.90	36 Kr 83.80
37 Rb 85.47	38 Sr 87.62	39 Y 88.91	40 Zr 91.22	41 Nb 92.91	42 Mo 95.94	43 Tc 98.91	44 Ru 101.1	45 Rh 102.9	46 Pd 106.4	47 Ag 107.9	48 Cd 112.4	49 In 114.8	50 Sn 118.7	51 Sb 121.8	52 Te 127.6	53 I 126.9	54 Xe 131.3
55 Cs 132.9	56 Ba 137.3	57 La 138.9	72 Hf 178.5	73 Ta 180.9	74 W 183.9	75 Re 186.2	76 Os 190.2	77 Ir 192.2	78 Pt 195.1	79 Au 197.0	80 Hg 200.6	81 Tl 204.4	82 Pb 207.2	83 Bi 209.0	84 Po (209)	85 At (210)	86 Rn (222)
87 Fr (223)	88 Ra 226.0	89 Ac 227.0	104 Rf (261)	105 Db (262)	106 Sg (263)	107 Bh (262)	108 Hs 	109 Mt 									

Lanthanide Series

58 Ce 140.1	59 Pr 140.9	60 Nd 144.2	61 Pm (145)	62 Sm 150.4	63 Eu 152.0	64 Gd 157.3	65 Tb 158.9	66 Dy 162.5	67 Ho 164.9	68 Er 167.3	69 Tm 168.9	70 Yb 173.0	71 Lu 175.0

Actinide Series

90 Th 232.0	91 Pa 231.0	92 U 238.0	93 Np 237.0	94 Pu (244)	95 Am (243)	96 Cm (247)	97 Bk (247)	98 Cf (251)	99 Es (252)	100 Fm (257)	101 Md (258)	102 No (259)	103 Lr (260)

1. The Puzzle

Almost all mystery books *end* with the solution. This mystery book begins with the solution. Here it is—on the facing page.

What on earth is it?

As it turns out, every material thing on earth—and in space as well.

This is the Periodic Table of the *Elements. It is the solution to the mystery of what every material thing is ultimately made of—trees, rocks, dirt, cells, plants, your hair, your skin, the clouds, the air, the sun, the moon, and the stars.

The asterisk indicates an item listed in the glossary.

1

Anything that has *mass and takes up space is made from some of the elements.

But what is an element?

Elementary means the first, the very beginning. The elements are the first things out of which every material thing else is made. When you get to these elements, you have gotten to the bottom of things— although not quite the very bottom, as we shall see in a later chapter.

Modern chemists define an element as a substance that cannot be broken down by chemical change into simpler, purer substances.

While salt is on your table, you won't find salt on the Table of Elements. Why? Salt can be broken down further, into Sodium and Chlorine. Sodium is found on the Table, designated by the chemical symbol "Na." Chlorine is designated by "Cl." When we have gotten to Sodium and Chlorine, as far as chemistry is concerned we have gotten to the bottom of things, and cannot go any further.

As you can see, there are 109 elements on our Periodic Table. Some are very common. Some are very rare. Some occur in nature. Some are manmade. As we shall see in a later chapter, some more elements can be added even beyond the 109 you see here— manmade elements, not natural elements. But for now, let's focus on the 109 we see on our Table.

A little over 98½% of the earth is made up of only 8 of these elements: Iron (Fe), Oxygen (O), Silicon (Si), Magnesium (Mg), Nickel (Ni), Sulfur (S), Calcium (Ca), and Aluminum (Al). Oxygen and Iron by themselves make up about 65% of the earth.

If we look at the entire universe, about 97% of it is made up of only 2 elements, the two on the very top left and top right side of the Periodic Table, Hydrogen (H) and Helium (He).

Some of these elements are seen every day, although not in their purest form. The coins in your pocket or purse are (for the most part) made of Copper (Cu), Nickel (Ni), Silver (Ag), and if you are really lucky or really rich, Gold (Au).

Most of the elements were not easy to find. On the contrary, they were very difficult to find. They had to be discovered, and they certainly were not found conveniently labeled and stacked in such neat rows as we find them on the Periodic Table of Elements.

Indeed, when we look at these nice, neat, and straight rows of elements we might think that it was a nice, neat, and straight road to their discovery. Nothing could be further from the truth. It was a long and difficult journey much like the perilous wanderings of Odysseus in Homer's great epic tale, the *Odyssey*. Of course, the wandering made it an adventure, and an adventure is always an exciting thing to retell.

2. The First Chemists?

Who were the first chemists? They were not scientists. They did not work in laboratories. They were workers of metal. They were not seeking to find out what the elements were, nor were they after truth for its own sake. They were quite practical men, interested in making beautiful jewelry and better weapons.

The ancient metal workers might be considered the very first chemists because instead of working with the elements in mixtures (as cloth dyers and medicine makers did), they worked with the pure elements, or to be exact, the pure metals.

In the pre-Christian era the ancients knew only seven basic metals: gold (Au), silver (Ag), copper (Cu), lead (Pb), tin (Sn), iron (Fe), and mercury (Hg).

Mercury was discovered last, about the 4th century BC. Which element was discovered first?

More blood has been shed over the very first element discovered, more kingdoms have risen and fallen, and more dreams have been conjured and shattered as well. There is no more useless element—certainly no more useless metal! It is too soft to make into any kind of durable tool or weapon, but it is more beautiful than any other element.

The first person to discover it probably caught sight of a luminous flash by the side of a riverbank while he was taking a walk. Curious, he walked over and dug it out with his toe, picked it up, and brushed this oddly heavy object off.

It was gold!

Gold is the metal that, more than any other, is found in a pure form, and often right out in the open. It is as if the most beautiful element was half-hidden by somebody, just waiting to be discovered. So brilliant, so glorious and pure, gold could not fail to attract man's attention. For that very reason, archaeologists have found gold ornaments dating all the way back to the Neolithic era (7000-4000 BC). But surely gold must have been noticed before that.

In any case, as the Neolithic men soon realized, gold makes a worthless hoe or spearhead. A common rock or stick would work better.

Gold is so soft that for thousands of years its use was purely decorative. And so while gold makes a very bad tool or weapon, it makes a breathtaking necklace or bracelet.

So back before there was writing, while people still used stone and wood tools, gold was known. And since gold was so soft, they could work it by pounding on it with stone tools. They did not even need fire.

It is also possible that silver and copper were known nearly as early, for while they are most likely to occur as *ores (that is, mixed with other elements), they sometimes do occur in nature in their pure form. But not nearly as much as gold.

Gold, silver, and copper might have been the only pure elements humanity ever found had it not been for a very important discovery, a discovery of something that is not itself an element, but without which it is quite unlikely that any other elements would ever have been isolated and discovered. Indeed, without it, chemistry would have been completely impossible.

Fire.

The discovery of fire transformed the entire history of humanity. Without fire, there would have been no civilization. There would have been no chemistry. There would be no Periodic Table of Elements because almost all the elements would have remained forever shrouded in mystery.

So maybe the real honor of the first chemist

should go to the person who first realized that fire *changed* what it heated.

Sometime during the Neolithic period, fire was first tamed, and with the taming of fire, the *smelting of metals became possible.

Smelting is necessary because most metals do not occur like gold (and sometimes silver and copper), in pure forms at or near the surface of the earth. They occur in the compounds called ores, the concentrated but impure deposits of metals in the earth's crust.

And by the way, we ought to be very thankful that such metal ores *do* occur in concentrated form. What if the metals were simply spread out uniformly in the earth's crust? We would never have found them! Or at least we never could have gathered enough gold, silver, copper, or any other metal to make anything.

Why?

Fill a glass container with a cup of sand. Add a *experiment* teaspoonful of pepper, and a teaspoonful of sugar. Shake it very well.

Could you get the pepper and sugar back out again? It might take a thousand years! We are fortunate indeed that metals are gathered together in concentrated deposits.

But even with the concentration of metals in ores near the earth's surface, we would not have gotten very much of any metal, not even of gold, without smelting.

In its simplest form, smelting is the heating of ores to separate the desired metal from the undesirable elements of the ore.

How was smelting first discovered?

Perhaps a young Sumerian saw lightning hit an eroded hillside containing iron ore, and when he ran up to investigate, he found a gnarled piece of iron.

Or it could have been a curious Egyptian who found that the rocks he had placed around his fire the night before had been changed by morning—the copper hidden in the ore had been extracted by the fire!

However it began, by about 3500 BC the development of pottery kilns allowed for fire to be enclosed, and enclosing fire allowed the heat to reach temperatures hot enough and controlled enough for smelting. Archaeologists have found many larger copper items from this era—bowls, plates, ornaments—which show us that significant amounts of copper were being derived by the smelting process. Soon enough, smelting was used to extract other metals as well, especially more of the precious metals silver and gold which also occur in ores.

The smelting of metal ores by fire caused a great revolution, perhaps the greatest humanity has ever experienced. Nearly everything made of metal throughout history has been made by smelting metal ores, because without smelting no one would ever have enough of any metal to make much of anything. If the process of smelting had never been discovered, there would not have been tools sturdy enough for any but the most primitive agriculture. Even more important, there would be no complex machines—not even machines that print books like this one!

If we look at the process of smelting from our perspective, almost five thousand years after its discovery, we would say that smelting separates the metal from the other elements in ore deposits by *reduction. Why? Smelting removes elements from the metal ore so that the pure metal remaining weighs *less* than it did before. The ore has been *reduced*.

For example, when iron ore is smelted with carbon—charcoal, for example—the carbon (C) first unites with oxygen (O) to make carbon monoxide (CO). (We'll use the symbols that chemists use today, where letters signify the elements being combined. Don't worry about the little numbers for now, but you should try to look up the elements on the Periodic Table, inside the back cover, so that you can become more familiar with their position.)

C + O_2 => CO
(Carbon) (Oxygen) (Carbon Monoxide)

Then the oxygen part of the ore (the O in Fe_2O_3) combines with carbon monoxide, and the result is pure iron (symbolized by "Fe") and carbon dioxide.

Fe_2O_3 + CO => Fe + CO_2
(Iron Oxide) (Carbon Monoxide) (Iron) (Carbon Dioxide)

Carbon combines with oxygen to make the carbon monoxide. Then carbon monoxide combines with the oxygen in iron oxide so that only the pure metal is left. Carbon is therefore called the *reducing agent*.

To help draw off other impurities, a *flux* is used to fuse the impurities together so they can be skimmed off the pure metal. For example, limestone ($CaCO_3$) is used as a flux in making iron to draw off the silica (SiO_2), one of the other impurities in the ore.

Now the first smelters of iron (or copper, or tin, or lead, or any of the other metals) knew nothing about such fancy chemical equations, nor even that the iron weighed less than the iron ore. They did not even know that oxygen existed.

But they did know that they could get pure copper by smelting *this* kind of ore, and pure tin by smelting *that* kind of ore, and so on with the rest of the metals.

They also learned that they could create new and stronger metals by mixing them—again, with the help of fire. Such mixtures are called *alloys.

The alloy bronze was created by mixing copper and tin. Bronze makes better tools and weapons, so much better that historians, looking back at the vast changes this mixture allowed, named the period from 3000 BC to 1200 BC the Bronze Age.

They learned that smelting iron ore with charcoal (adding more carbon to the iron than could combine with the oxygen in the ore) created an even stronger metal, the alloy we call steel. And again, the change was so important that the time after 1200 BC has been called the Iron Age by historians.

So the ancients not only gathered seven metals by smelting, a process of *separation*, but also created new metals by *combination*.

Little did the ancients know how large a step they had made toward the science of chemistry. Separation moves the chemist closer to the fundamental elements. Combination allows him to create new and better substances. Separation and combination are the two essential processes of chemistry, and that is why the metal workers deserve the name of the first chemists.

Prior to the birth of Christ, then, our Periodic Table had seven elements, the seven metals. Actually, it had two more, since the ancients knew about sulfur (S), but called it brimstone, and carbon (C) in the form of diamonds and charcoal. So we may fill in nine of the elements. Only 100 more to be discovered!

But we must be very clear about something. The ancients did not *know* that these were the elements. They did not know they were fundamental. Most thought the real elements were Earth, Air, Fire, and Water, and everything else—including gold, silver, copper, iron, lead, tin, mercury, sulfur, and carbon—was made out of them.

3. Earth, Air, Fire, and Water

For much of history the "Table of Elements," if we can call it that, was very simple.

Earth (E), air (A), fire (F), and water (W). Think how easy a test in chemistry would be!

A slightly more complex Table might look like this:

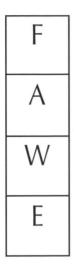

The relation of the elements, top to bottom, represents their weight. Earth is heaviest and fire is lightest. Or, to be more exact, fire isn't heavy at all. It doesn't have any weight. It's simply lightness!

The Ionian philosopher Anaximander [an AXE ih man der], who lived in the sixth century BC, was the first to argue that these were the four elements, and the belief that these were the fundamental elements lasted about two thousand years. To be more exact, Anaximander argued that there were four "opposites" out of which everything was made: hot, cold, dry, and moist. But these four were identified with fire, earth, air, and water respectively. We find the same teaching in Empedocles [em PED uh klees] a century later. (He was born on the island of Sicily.)

Some thought that one of these was *the* fundamental element, and the rest were somehow made out of it. Thales [THAY leez], a philosopher from Asia Minor, who may have been the teacher of Anaximander, thought that everything was ultimately made of water.

Anaximenes [an axe ih MEN eez], who lived at the same time and in the same place as Anaximander, thought that air was *the* element, and fire was expanded air, water was compressed air, and earth was even more tightly compressed air.

Heraclitus [hair uh KLY tuss], a philosopher born in Ephesus who lived about the same time as Anaximander and Anaximenes, thought that fire was the fundamental element, and that air was contracted fire, water was contracted air, and earth was contracted water.

Variations of these beliefs—often very elaborate variations—are found sprinkled throughout the next two thousand years.

But there was another approach, that of Democritus [dih MOCK rih tuss], a Thracian born in the 5th century BC, Epicurus [ep ih CURE us], a Greek born on the island of Samos in the 4th century, and Lucretius [lew CREE shuss], a 1st century BC Roman. They thought that everything, including earth, water, air, and fire was actually made of tiny uncuttable bits of colorless, smell-less, tasteless matter which differed only in shape and size. The Greek word for uncuttable is *atomos*. These men were the atomists, and we shall come back to their view in later chapters.

Finally, there was Aristotle. In many important respects Aristotle agreed with Anaximander. He too believed that there were four opposite *elements* (hot, cold, moist, and dry) out of which were made the simple *bodies* (fire, air, water, and earth). The relationship between the elements and the simple bodies could be put in a rather ingenious square chart.

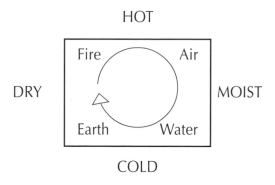

Each simple body was made of two elements. Fire was made of the dry and the hot. Air was made of the hot and moist. Water was made of the moist and cold. Finally—and I am sure that you have seen the pattern by now—earth was made from the cold and the dry.

Furthermore, the simple bodies changed into one another by exchanging elements, an exchange which allowed for a kind of cyclical pattern in nature.

Fire (dry + hot) changed into air (moist + hot) by keeping the hot but changing from dry to moist.

And air (moist + hot) could then change into water (moist + cold) by keeping the moist but changing from hot to cold.

This pattern of change eventually brought fire, air, water, and earth into a kind of cycle of change, ending up right back at fire again, for earth (dry + cold) could change into fire (dry + hot) by changing from cold to hot.

What about everything else? What about gold, silver, and lead? What about trees, and cows, and grass?

These were all thought to be made from various combinations of all four of the simple bodies. Each of the visible things—including our own bodies— were made up of earth, air, fire, and water.

It is important to understand, however, that Aristotle did not think that merely adding up earth, air, fire, and water in different combinations would automatically create gold, or a tree, or a human being. He argued that even the simple bodies themselves had to have a *form* that unified the material parts into a whole.

Just as letters do not make a word until you *form* them into a word, so also for Aristotle fire, air, earth, and water did not make a piece of gold, or a cabbage, or a cat, or a human being without the *form* of gold, or a cabbage, or a cat, or a human being. Each thing was a unity of form and matter.

Now we must admit that we are making Aristotle's account of nature far simpler than it actually was. But at least we have an idea of the kind of argument he made about the elements and the simple bodies.

In one sense this approach lasted a very long time, about two millennia, that is, about two thousand years. Most seekers into the things of nature for a long time after Aristotle considered the four elements to be hot, cold, moist, and dry, and the four simple bodies to be fire, air, water, and earth. Or, they got a bit sloppy, and thought as some before Aristotle had done, that fire, air, water, and earth themselves were the elements.

But as we have seen with the metal workers, even before the general belief in the four elements came about, fire was being used to take earth apart into more fundamental things. (Not earth in the pure sense, however. Aristotle and others like him thought that the everyday earth under your feet was a mixture of some or all of the four bodies, with pure earth being the predominant part.)

Oddly enough, theoretical knowledge (how we *think* about things) was going in the opposite direction from practice (how things are *done*).

Aristotle *thought* the seven known metals came *from* earth, air, fire, and water, or to be more exact, he thought that the metals all came from vaporous exhalations (somewhat like steam) in the earth being compressed, dried, and hence solidified. But for Aristotle, gold, silver, copper, and the rest of the metals were not elements. They came *from* the elements.

Whether the very practical metal worker thought about what he was doing at all, he was indeed changing what he found in the earth (that is, metal ore) into pure elements like gold, silver, copper, and so on. By smelting with fire, he was *reducing* earth (a compound) to an element. In practice, then, the metal worker was getting us closer to being a chemist and closer to the Periodic Table.

Next we shall go to the alchemists, who were *thinking* like Aristotle but *acting* like metal workers.

4. The Alchemists

While the smelters of metals were after very practical things, the alchemists were fascinated with the mysteries of nature herself. Why? Because they, exactly like the philosophers before them and the modern day scientists who came after them, loved a mystery, and the love of such knowledge drove them into the laboratory—the very first laboratories, to be exact.

But we must admit that they were after more than knowledge for its own sake. They were on a treasure hunt as well, looking for the secret by which base metals could be turned into gold. So, in the end, some of the alchemists had at least one eye on the profit which could be had from their art. But most, it seems, wanted the knowledge of how nature worked more than they wanted the gold.

As we have seen, the smelting of metals by fire goes all the way back several thousand years before the birth of Christ. Alchemy, however, began in the first century BC, most probably in Egypt. Indeed, scholars believe that the "chem" in alchemy (and hence in chemistry) is from a Coptic word "khem" which means the Black Land, that is, Egypt, for after the Nile River rises and floods the land each year, it looks black. That alchemy probably began in Egypt makes sense. The Egyptians were some of the best metal workers of the ancient world.

From Egypt, alchemy spread to the Greek-speaking world, to Syria, and then to Persia. When Islam arose in the 7th and 8th centuries AD, it became the main bearer of alchemy. Indeed, the name alchemy comes from the Arabic. Al means "the" in Arabic, so al-chemy, is "the art of the black land."

With the spread of Islam all around the Mediterranean Sea, alchemy spread as well, and reached the Latin-speaking west in the 12th century.

Of course, the alchemists knew the seven basic metals, but they thought about them in a much grander way than the metal workers. The alchemists associated each of the metals with a day of the week and a planet. Each metal also had a symbol, and the symbols were used for many centuries after. They were the first chemical symbols, and the alchemists wrote chemical formulae with them. Now you know why wizards in stories often have big hats with some of the following symbols stitched all over them—alchemists were thought to be wizards!

Gold	Sunday	Sun	☉
Silver	Monday	Moon	☽
Iron	Tuesday	Mars	♂
Mercury	Wednesday	Mercury	☿
Tin	Thursday	Jupiter	♃
Copper	Friday	Venus	♀
Lead	Saturday	Saturn	♄

The relationship between the planets and the days Sun-day and Moon-day is obvious. As for the rest, the Saxon god Tiw is the same as the Roman war god Mars, hence we call it Tiw's-day, instead of Mars-day. The Saxon god Woden is the same as Mercury, and so we call it Woden's-day instead of Mercury-day. Thursday was named for the god Thor, rather than for Jupiter. And finally Friff (the wife of Woden) took the place of Venus for the Saxons, and so we have Friff-day, or Friday.

But what about the relationship of the planets to the metals? The sun is golden, and the moon silvery.

Mercury, or quicksilver, was a good element for the planet Mercury, which seemed to move the fastest. Lead was a good element for Saturn, the planet that appeared to move the slowest. Iron when it rusts is red, and Mars is red. Further, the war god must certainly use iron for his sword and spearpoint. The others? We aren't quite sure. The alchemists were a secretive lot.

Again, the most important goal for the alchemist was the knowledge of how to turn base metals (such as lead or mercury) into gold. We recall that Aristotle thought that the metals were made from compressed vaporous exhalations under the ground. The alchemists, basing themselves upon Aristotle, identified the dry vapor with sulfur (a non-metal) and the moist vapor with mercury (a metal), and thought that these two combined within the earth to create all the other metals. All that had to be done—so it seemed to them—was recreate the way the gold had been produced under the ground, but do it *above* ground, in the laboratory. Perhaps that is why alchemists' laboratories resembled dark, dank, and smoky caverns!

In their effort to ply nature for her secrets—and produce gold in the process—alchemists came up with a dazzling variety of strange instruments and concoctions.

We would find a good many familiar and some unfamiliar instruments in an alchemist's laboratory. There would be large round-bottomed flasks and

smaller bottles, funnels and filters, great metal vats
and furnaces, mortars and pestles, and scales. All
very familiar.

But we would also find all kinds of oddly shaped
devices. One of the most important was the alembic, a glass device which looks like a squat bird with
a tremendous long, thin beak.

Distillation of pure water (O) from saltwater solution (XOXO)

The alembic was used for *distillation*, a very important process of chemistry right down to the
present day. Distilling is somewhat like the process
of reduction used in smelting in that it separates
substances that consist of more than one element,
into simpler (or "purer") substances. But in distilling, the separation does not occur because of a

chemical reaction (like the removal of oxygen from metal ore with carbon monoxide). The separation occurs by vaporizing (using the heat of a fire) or evaporating (using the heat of the sun) one part of the compound from another. As long as one part of the compound vaporizes or evaporates more easily than the other, distillation can be used to separate them.

So, for example, if you wanted to get pure water from saltwater, you could distill the salt water. You can make a very simple distillation apparatus to do just that. Add one tablespoon of salt to three cups of water. Stir until the salt completely dissolves. Taste it. Then put the saltwater into a pan. Put a curved cover on it, and heat until it boils. Let it boil for a minute, then pull the pan lid off, turn it over quickly, and let it cool. Taste the liquid which has condensed and gathered on the lid. It's no longer saltwater, but pure water. You have distilled water from saltwater.

While the alchemist's instruments may look quite unlike the sophisticated and shining instruments of today's chemist, today's chemist stands on the shoulders, so to speak, of the alchemist. For in the long, difficult process of discovering the elements, the alchemists' tools allowed for the beginnings of the kinds of processes by which the elements were eventually identified.

Some people have the right idea, but go about it the wrong way. The alchemists had the wrong idea (that they could turn lead into gold), but went about it in the right way (discovering the right processes for later chemists). In fact, the alchemists invented almost all of the chemical apparatus used up until the 17th century.

Yet it was not just instruments that made an alchemist, but his concoctions as well. Not only was he busy designing various kinds of devices, but he was also brewing various mixtures by which he hoped that he could bring about the desired goal of transforming base metals into gold.

And so we might find on his shelf some vitriol of Cyprus (copper sulfate), white vitriol (zinc sulfate), aqua regia (nitro-hydrochloric acid), arsenic, saltpeter (potassium nitrate), alum of Yemen (aluminium sulphate), burning water (alcohol), brimstone (sulfur) or sal ammoniac (ammonium chloride).

We should note that only two of the chemicals listed are elements: sulfur (S) and arsenic (As). The alchemists did not discover many pure elements. They thought they *already* knew what the elements were: hot, dry, cold, and moist (or fire, earth, air, and water). It is very hard to find something if you think you've already discovered it—especially if you are mistaken, that is!

But they did something else very important which would allow later scientists to discover the real elements. The alchemists collected all kinds of strange chemical compounds, and very carefully recorded how they reacted to being heated in various ways (either by themselves, or with other compounds). That was a step in the right direction.

Some of the most important substances discovered by the alchemists' misbegotten attempts at creating gold were *acids (mainly sulfuric, hydrochloric, and nitric acids). The word acid comes from the Latin *acidus*, which means "sour," an appropriate name, since acids (in water solutions) do taste sour.

Acids have all kinds of strange and wonderful effects, and are especially helpful in breaking substances down—the ultimate goal of the chemist. To get to the bottom of things, to find the ultimate, simple elements, we have to take apart the more complex, everyday substances. Acids help take them apart (and sometimes put them together) in strange, and mysterious ways.

Here is one such mysterious way. Put 3 Tablespoons of vinegar into a tall glass. Then add 1 teaspoon of baking soda. (You should do this on the kitchen counter, so you can easily mop up the mess!)

Exactly what happened? Where did all the bubbles come from? Was there air trapped in the vinegar? In the baking soda? In both?

If you can, do the same experiment with a small-necked bottle and a balloon. Put the vinegar into the bottle, pour in a tablespoon of baking soda, and quickly put the balloon over the top of the bottle.

Now we are sure that air, somehow, is being produced or released from the ingredients. How do we know? The volume of air increased; that is, the total amount of air increased.

Original volume of air = air in bottle

New volume of air = air in bottle + air in balloon

If we could measure the volume of the air, we could make an equation so that we would know how much air we produced by adding different amounts of vinegar and soda.

3 Tablespoons vinegar + 1 Tablespoon baking soda = volume of air in balloon

Vinegar is an acid, one with which the alchemists were very familiar. (Although, to be exact, vinegar *contains* an acid, acetic acid: $HC_2H_3O_2$.) In any case, you can be sure that the alchemists did many experiments much like the one you just performed. Such experiments produced something that you caught, but the alchemists did *not* see even though it was right in front of their noses (or under their beards, as the case may be). Their blindness to it kept them from advancing in the knowledge of nature.

What did they miss?

Air.

Not only did they not have a way to trap the air that escaped from the chemical reactions, but they didn't think it worth their notice.

So while the alchemists took us a long way toward chemistry and the Periodic Table, the end was still far off. Oddly enough, the key to unlocking the mystery of the elements, and hence the mystery of the Periodic Table, was the discovery of the strange and marvelous properties of air. But that would take some time and quite a bit of effort, as we shall soon see.

VAN HELMONT

5. "This Spirit, Hitherto Unknown"

The alchemists worked feverishly, day and night, with different liquids and solids, which they took to be different forms of water and earth. Yet they completely overlooked air. Oddly, the advance of chemical knowledge was hindered by the ignorance of something that is everywhere, but cannot be seen.

Of course, they knew that there *was* air. But they did not direct their attention to it. Alchemy could not be transformed into chemistry until the efforts of the alchemists were turned to an examination of air.

Who first turned to air? Johann Baptista van Helmont (1579-1644), a man half alchemist and half chemist. Actually, he was called an *iatrochemist.* An iatrochemist? Merely a fancy term for someone who applied the knowledge and procedures developed by the alchemists to the cure of diseases rather than to the production of gold. (The Greek word for "healer" is *iatros.*)

To be more exact, Helmont did not attempt to examine air itself, but discovered *gas* (which he thought ultimately came from water). In this, he was a bit like that ancient Greek philosopher Thales, who thought everything came from water. In contrast to Thales, Helmont believed that there were two elements, air and water, but like Thales he thought that everything *except* the air ultimately came from water.

How did he prove that everything came from water?

By a very ingenious experiment—an experiment which he carried out in a very careful way.

In a large container, Helmont put 200 pounds of earth which he had first dried out in a furnace. He then planted a willow tree weighing 5 pounds in the dirt. He kept the dirt covered so not even any dust could enter the container. Over the next five years, Helmont watered the willow tree, using only rainwater or distilled water.

At the end of five years he weighed the tree: 169 pounds and 3 ounces. He also dried the dirt in the furnace again. It weighed just three ounces less than the original 200 pounds.

There we have it! The tree must have gained over 164 pounds *from the addition* of *water alone*! What else could have caused it? Thales must have been right!

JOHANN BAPTISTA
VAN HELMONT

As it turns out, neither Thales nor Helmont were right. We shall return to this experiment in a few moments. But first, let us witness another, in which Helmont discovered gas.

Helmont took 62 pounds of charcoal (charcoal is burned wood), and heated it in the open air. He was left with only 1 pound of ash. The rest? It escaped—as *spiritus silvestre*, "spirit of wood."

He repeated the experiment, this time enclosing the charcoal in a vessel. The escaping gas shattered the vessel. *Spiritus silvestre* also means "wild spirit," since wild things live in the woods, and this was certainly a wild and powerful spirit.

"I call this spirit, hitherto unknown, by the new name of *gas*," declared Helmont boldly.

The word "gas" he derived from the Greek word "chaos" which means "formless mass." Helmont called this strange spirit a gas because it did not have a shape of its own nor could he keep it in a container.

What exactly did he think gas was, then? Formless water—and that will take a bit of explaining. Helmont thought that everything was made out of water, but that water was itself formless. What gives it form? "Ferments," he answered. Ferments were somewhat like Aristotle's forms, an organizing principle of matter. For Helmont, ferments formed water into definite things in nature. If the ferments were destroyed, the water was formless again, and the formless water he called "gas."

Many of the elements on the Periodic Table are still called gases, such as hydrogen (H), oxygen (O), and nitrogen (N). Of course, chemists do not now believe in Helmont's "ferments," and so do not believe that gas is ferment-less water. Today, we understand gas to be one of the four possible *states* of matter: solid, liquid, gas, and plasma. Water, for example, can exist as a solid (when it is frozen), as a liquid, and as a gas (when it is boiled). But oxygen, which exists normally as a gas, can also be turned into a liquid. Just cool it to minus 183 degrees Celsius—183 degrees below the freezing point of water! (Plasma, the fourth state, consisting of charged gaseous particles, does not naturally exist on earth, except in lightning.)

But Helmont was not quite seeing things this way. Although he went on to discover and name many different gases, for him, all of these gases ultimately came from water. The spirit of wood, for example, obviously came from the wood, and as we have already seen him prove, the tree came from water.

Therefore, the gas must have come from water. Impeccable logic!

Well, rather peccable logic as it turns out, for one's logic is only as good as one's observations. What was spirit of wood—as we understand it today, that is? The very same gas that made his willow tree grow: carbon dioxide (CO_2).

In his second experiment, the carbon (C) in the charcoal combined with oxygen (O) in the air to make carbon dioxide (CO_2). The volume of the newly-created carbon dioxide, as a gas, was larger than the vessel would allow. Boom!

In his first experiment, the willow tree was not just taking in water, but also (from the air) carbon dioxide (CO_2) as well. By a process called photosynthesis, the tree was turning carbon dioxide into sugar that, along with other organic compounds, make up the cells of the tree. It would be closer to the truth to say that the tree was built out of air! (Not very much closer, however.)

But Helmont could not understand either of these things. No one could at the time.

Oxygen had not been discovered yet. Neither had photosynthesis. Nor did he have the kind of containers and instruments that could trap and measure the gases accurately.

He would have been very surprised to find that water and air, which he thought were the only two elements, were actually made up of *more fundamental* elements. He would have been even more surprised to find out that water (H_2O) came from two gases, hydrogen (H) and oxygen (O), rather than that the gases came from water.

And so, as with the alchemists, Helmont had the wrong ideas (that gases came from water), yet went about it in the right way (by compiling a long list of chemical reactions which produced various gases). But chemistry could only advance toward the Periodic Table when air and water were analyzed into their constituent elements, that is, into gases.

6. *The Atomists Return*

Robert Boyle (1627-1691) was the 14th child of Richard Boyle, the first Earl of Cork. (Cork is a county on the southern coast of Ireland.) His father, the Earl, was very rich, and even though his fortune seemed to bob up and down like a cork floating on a choppy sea, Robert was able to inherit a large amount of money.

The sons of some rich men often throw away all their money on racehorses, or fancy clothes, or other frivolous things. Not Robert Boyle. He used his money as a scientist, building his laboratory and buying chemical supplies. He was a passionate scientist indeed.

When young Robert was about 14 years old, he traveled to Florence, Italy, where he was introduced to the ideas of the great astronomer and mathematician Galileo Galilei (who had just died). While it was the last year of Galileo's life, it was the first year, we might say, of Robert Boyle's scientific life.

What did he learn from Galileo's writings which so ignited his mind?

Two things.

The first was a new view of nature, a view that was really very old, the atomism of Democritus, Epicurus, and Lucretius, which (we recall) is the view that everything in the universe was made of bits of colorless, smell-less, tasteless matter differing only in size and shape. The ancient texts of Democritus, Epicurus, and Lucretius had been rediscovered in the 15th and 16th centuries, and the atomistic view spread all over Europe by the 17th century. Boyle was to learn much more about atomism from two Frenchmen living during Boyle's time, Pierre Gassendi and Rene Descartes, but he got his start from Galileo's work.

The second thing he learned from Galileo's writings was the use of mathematics in astronomy (the study of the stars and planets) and dynamics (the study of the motions of material bodies).

Our interest is only in Boyle's acceptance of atomism. Although Boyle was not the first modern atomist—again, interest in atomism had been fairly strong since the 16th century—he was the first who tried to apply the theory of atomism directly to the subject matter of the alchemists and iatrochemists. It was the revival of this ancient theory that helped to turn chemistry back toward the right direction, toward the elements in the Periodic Table, and away from earth, air, fire, and water as fundamental.

Aristotle had thought that atomism was wrong, and he rejected the views of the ancient Greek atomist Democritus. (The other atomists, Epicurus and Lucretius, lived after Aristotle.) But Boyle thought that Aristotle was wrong, and so he rejected the alchemists' belief (based on Aristotle) that fire, earth, air, and water were the fundamental elements, and Aristotle's belief that each thing had a definite form. Instead, Boyle believed that everything was made of atoms—including fire, earth, air, and water—and that a thing's "form" was merely the result of how the atoms were put together.

What exactly did he think atoms were?

For Boyle, there was really only *one* physical substance, which he called "universal matter," and it was broken up into the smallest of pieces. These pieces of matter Boyle thought were indestructible.

For Boyle, matter had three properties: motion, size, and shape. If the pieces of different size and shape were put together in one way, they made gold.

If they were put together in another way, they might make silver.

Or lead.

Or sulfur.

Or, in more complicated ways, any physical thing, like a leaf, or a tree, or even the human body.

But no matter how different things *appeared* to be, deep down, on the smallest, microscopic level, the "stuff" out of which they were made was exactly the same, atoms.

There are several interesting things to note here.

First of all, if *every* thing was made of *one* thing, then we should be able to take apart this *thing* and make it into *that* thing—just as a child can take apart a building he has made of wooden blocks and make a bridge instead. As we said, Boyle thought atoms were like wooden blocks—different in shape and size, but still all made of the very same thing. That meant, of course, that Boyle thought that lead (or anything else, for that matter) could be turned into gold, just as the alchemists had.

Second, while Boyle did turn chemistry in the right direction so that chemists would look for elements more fundamental than earth, air, fire, and water, he overshot the mark, speeding right past the real elements (such as gold, silver, lead, and so on) and directly to atoms. Atoms were his elements, and gold, silver and so on were, for Boyle, merely combinations of the elemental atoms.

Yet, we should add, he did allow that some combinations of particular kinds of atoms were far more durable than others. These more durable combinations he called "primary concretions," which, "though not absolutely indivisible by nature" like the atoms, yet "very rarely happen to be actually dissolved or broken, but remain entire in great variety of sensible bodies, and under various forms or disguises." These "primary concretions" correspond roughly to the notion of the elements in our Periodic Table, and allowed Boyle as a chemist to treat gold, silver, lead, arsenic, and so on, as if they were quasielemental, which is a fancy way to say "more or less like elements."

In a way, then, Boyle was, more or less, on the right track, even though he was speeding. (He should have heeded that old Latin saying, *festina lente*, "make haste slowly.") As we shall see in a later chapter, we have since found out that there is a different kind of atom for each element (rather than elements being made out of several atoms of different shapes and sizes, as Boyle thought). But more to the point, Boyle was too quick to jump over the problem of discovering the elements and leap into the atomic world. As we shall see, chemists had to focus on discovering the elements themselves *before* they could know anything at all about atoms and their structure. First things first.

Third and last—and related to the second point— we should realize that Boyle could not possibly have *seen* whether he was right or not. He certainly *thought* he was right about atoms, but microscopes had only just been invented during his lifetime, and they were not very powerful at all. It was about four centuries later that microscopes became powerful enough even to begin to peer into the atomic world, and the atoms scientists found were not, as we shall see, very much like what Boyle had imagined. In the meantime, however, chemists could both see and experiment on the elements.

If we turn from theory to practice, we find that Robert Boyle was a very good practical scientist, and he discovered many wonderful things.

For example, the relationship between the pressure and volume of a gas. If you *increase* the pressure on a gas trapped in a container, the volume of the gas (that is, the space it takes up) will *decrease* proportionately. Boyle found out, through many experiments, that the volume of a gas is *inversely proportional* to the pressure. ("Inversely proportional" simply means that as one increases, the other decreases in the same way.) This relationship is now called "Boyle's Law."

For example, if you *double* the pressure, the space which the gas takes up will be half of what it was.

If you *triple* the pressure, the space which the gas takes up will be $1/3$ of what it was.

If you *quadruple* the pressure? It will take up $1/4$ of the space, of course.

He also discovered a way to test for acids and bases, a very important thing for chemists right down to the present day. Before Boyle, the only way to identify an acid was that it effervesced (bubbled) when a *base, its chemical opposite, was added to it, and the only way to identify a base was that it effervesced when an acid was added to it. But that, of course, is not very helpful. How could you tell which was which? Worse yet, metals effervesce when acids are added to them, and metals are not bases.

But Boyle devised a way to tell the *difference* between an acid and a base. He found that the purple juice of violets (which he got by boiling the petals) turned red if it was dropped into an acid, and blue if it was dropped into a base.

You can try the same thing, and use the juice of purple cabbage instead (which you get by boiling several cabbage leaves in 3-4 cups of water for about 15 minutes). We recall that in the experiment at the end of Chapter 4, vinegar was an acid, reacting with baking soda. Baking soda was a base (or alkali, as it is sometimes called). If you put a few drops of purple cabbage juice into some vinegar, and a few drops into a solution of baking soda and water, you will find that the vinegar turns red, and the baking soda solution turns green. Scientists use this test today, and it is called a litmus test. Litmus paper is soaked in a vegetable dye derived from lichens, and then dried. When the paper is dipped in acid, it turns from pink to red, and when dipped in a base, turns blue. (Thus, we normally think of blue as the test color for bases, but as we see from the cabbage juice, different chemicals can cause different test colors.)

He also did many experiments with the newly invented vacuum pump (in fact, so many that fellow British referred to the vacuum as the *vacuum Boylianum*). When he pumped all the air out of a glass globe, he found that a candle would immediately snuff out, and the smoke of the extinguished candle would fall down, instead of rise. He found that a mouse placed in the glass globe would suffocate. He did not know it, but he was showing that a candle cannot burn and an animal cannot breathe without oxygen.

Boyle also did important experiments showing that when metal is heated in the open air it *gains weight*, a process called *calcination* because of the whitish substance that forms on the metal. (*Calx* is Latin for lime or chalk.) Why did it gain weight? Boyle thought that when metal was heated, "igneous corpuscles" (that is, atoms of fire!) were absorbed by the metal. Again, he could not know it, but it was actually oxygen from the air that caused the metal to gain weight.

He could not know about oxygen in either case simply because oxygen had not been discovered yet, and the discovery of oxygen was a very difficult thing, as we shall soon see.

PHLOGISTON

GEORG STAHL

7. The Strange Tale
of Phlogiston,
the Element That Wasn't

Before we can talk about the discovery of oxygen,
we need to examine a very strange substance that led
to the discovery of oxygen. This substance, named
phlogiston, was not real. It existed only in the minds
of those who believed in it, and some of the greatest
chemists in the 18th century thought it was very real.

We might say that these scientists got things exactly backwards. When they thought that phlogiston

was *added* to something, the truth was that oxygen had been *removed*, and when they thought that phlogiston had been *removed*, the truth was that oxygen had been *added*. But they could not know that because oxygen had not yet been discovered.

The very odd thing, however, is that the belief in phlogiston allowed these scientists to perform all kinds of very fruitful experiments. And we might even say that oxygen never would have been discovered if scientists had not spent so much effort in trying to understand phlogiston. Sometimes a clearly defined error is the only way to discover the truth.

And here is another odd thing. The very man most often credited with the discovery of oxygen, Joseph Priestley, died believing that he had actually shown, once and for all, that phlogiston existed and oxygen did not. He was like Christopher Columbus, who believed that he had actually landed in India, when he had really discovered America.

But on to the story.

This strange element-that-wasn't, phlogiston, began with a very strange man named Johann Joachim Becher [BECK er] (1635-1682). Becher was born in Speyer, Germany, and started out as a poor man who had a very rich imagination. When he was young, he was too poor to buy books, so he stole or borrowed them instead. He studied everything— theology, medicine, chemistry, politics, and law. He tried to create a universal language, one language which everyone could speak, but the man who paid him to do it, rejected it. He somehow managed to convince the Dutch government that he could turn sand into gold, but the sand remained sand. He attempted to make a perpetual motion machine, a clock, which would go on forever but he could not get the clock to start. He gained fame as an economist, even though his business ventures tended to go bankrupt. Alas, most of his schemes ended in failure.

JOHANN BECHER

(He introduced the potato into Germany to feed its pigs and cattle, and hungry peasants as well—that worked!)

So Becher was indeed a man of many talents, but very few successes. His greatest success was the introduction of the false theory of phlogiston. One of his followers, Georg Ernst Stahl [SHTAL] (1660-1734), born in Ansbach, Bavaria, was a great popularizer of Becher's views. He must have done a good job. Chemists believed in phlogiston for over a hundred years, and it was difficult to get them to change their minds. Some never did.

What made Becher, Stahl, and all the other chemists believe in phlogiston?

For Becher, there were three kinds of earth which, along with air and water, made up all bodies. One of the kinds of earth he named *terra pinguis*, or "fatty earth." Stahl renamed it φλογιστον—which he wrote in these Greek letters, for the Greek word φλογιστον (phlogiston) means "burned" or "set on fire." Both of them thought that anything that could be burned had this mysterious element in it. Phlogiston was the principle, or cause, of fire.

How did they prove it?

Even the alchemists had known that when a metal (zinc, for example) is heated red hot in the open air, a residue forms on it. As we recall from our chapter on Mr. Boyle, the metal with residue on it was called a calx (for example, calx of zinc). The really interesting thing, however, was that if the metal calx was again heated, but this time with charcoal, the metal was magically restored to its original condition!

A marvelous trick, but a mysterious one. What was going on? Becher and Stahl thought they knew.

To keep with our example, when zinc was originally burned in the open air, it turned bright red. "*That* is the phlogiston escaping!" they declared. After the phlogiston escaped, only calx of zinc was left.

Zinc + Fire => Calx of Zinc + Escaped Phlogiston

But they also found that the process could be reversed by heating the calx of zinc with charcoal. "Aha!" they reasoned, "the charcoal must be rich in phlogiston!" The charcoal must be giving its phlogiston to the calx of zinc which had lost it. When the calx of zinc gets its phlogiston back, of course it changes right back into zinc again.

Calx of Zinc + Charcoal [rich in phlogiston] => Zinc

Now there was one very odd thing about this equation: the calx of zinc *weighed more* than the zinc (as Boyle had noted with other metals). How could that be?

If zinc *lost* phlogiston by heating, then it should *weigh less* than it did before.

That was perplexing indeed. How could it be explained?

Boyle, we recall, thought that fire atoms had been added. But that answer would not work for Becher and Stahl because they were not atomists, and furthermore, they believed that phlogiston had escaped (rather than anything being added).

Some followers of Becher and Stahl thought that phlogiston might actually weigh less than nothing, so that when phlogiston is added to something, it *weighs less* than it did before.

What was actually happening?

When zinc (or most any metal) is heated in *air*, the metal *gains* oxygen from the air, so that the new substance, zinc oxide (which they called calx of zinc), is heavier by the amount of oxygen it has gained. When it is heated again with charcoal, the carbon in the charcoal takes the oxygen back out of the zinc oxide, and the zinc is restored to its original condition.

So that what actually happened was this.

Zinc + fire + air (containing Oxygen) => Zinc Oxide
(calx of zinc)

And when the process was reversed . . .

Zinc Oxide + Carbon (charcoal) = Zinc + Carbon Dioxide

But, as we said above, no one could know this until oxygen was discovered, and that required the diligent attempt to trap the phlogiston in a container so that it could be examined properly.

It was by setting a trap for phlogiston that they caught oxygen instead! Hydrogen was also found. Even more interesting, chemists found that water was made up of oxygen and hydrogen, two gases.

Here is the irony, however. The two men who found hydrogen and oxygen, and also found that the two combined to make water, did not believe in either hydrogen or oxygen. These men, Mr. Priestley and Mr. Cavendish, called oxygen *dephlogisticated air*—that is, air with the phlogiston taken out of it—and thought that hydrogen might actually be phlogiston. Perfectly marvelous errors, as we'll now see.

JOSEPH PRIESTLY

8. *Mr. Priestley Clears Things Up (Sort of)*

The first man we have already mentioned, Joseph Priestley (1733-1804). Priestley was born near Leeds, England. He did not start out to be a scientist at all, but a minister. Yet he also studied mathematics, astronomy, and a little chemistry. It was not until he met that famous American Benjamin Franklin while both happened to be in London that he decided to devote himself to science (although he remained a minister all his life too).

Franklin was honored in Europe for his scientific work with electricity, and Priestley was inspired by Franklin to write a history of electricity. But the more Priestley studied, the more difficulties, confusions, and disagreements he found among the scientists. Things only got worse as he branched out into the study of chemistry. He decided that he would have to clear things up. So it was that Priestley became a passionate scientist.

While everyone in Leeds was out enjoying the fresh air, where was Mr. Priestley? At the brewery next to his house, hanging his head over a great bubbling vat of brewing beer, testing the gas given off.

It extinguished a burning stick. Could it be the *gas sylvestre* of Helmont? Priestley had to know, but he needed to find a way to trap the gas to test it. He built his own laboratory to do just that.

Now trapping gas might seem a difficult thing to do, but Priestley found an excellent way of doing it. Although it was an Anglican minister Stephen Hales (1677-1761) who invented the "pneumatic trough," it was Priestley who perfected it.

"Pneumatic trough" is a fancy name for a very simple device. In fact, it is so simple that you can make one right now. All you need is a drinking glass and a soda straw (a bendable one if possible).

Fill your kitchen sink or a large bowl with about 3-4 inches of water. Fill a drinking glass to the very brim with water. Place a piece of cardboard over the glass. Holding the cardboard tightly over the glass, quickly (but carefully) turn the glass upside down and submerge the rim of the glass about an inch into the water in the sink. Remove the cardboard. There you have it: a pneumatic trough!

That's it? Well, not quite. Take the drinking straw, slip it under the upside down rim of the glass (without letting the rim above the surface of the water), and blow air into the upside down glass. Note that the exhaled gas displaces the water in the glass.

Priestley did much the same thing. He placed glass tubes filled with liquid (sometimes water, sometimes mercury) upside down on a little trough in a container filled with the same liquid. Other smaller curved tubing ran from

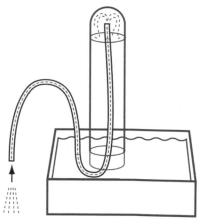

Pneumatic trough with air (or any gas) displacing water (or another liquid) in the glass

his experimental vessel beside the pneumatic trough, down into the liquid, and up into the upside down glass tubes. The gas given off during chemical reactions in the vessels could then run through the tube and be trapped in the upside down containers in the trough. Since the gas was lighter than the water, it rose to the top of the glass tube. The gas was trapped!

Priestley began to trap all kinds of gases given off by every kind of mixture he could devise. In his most famous experiment, Priestley isolated oxygen, although, again, he called it "dephlogisticated air." Why did he call it that?

Let us look at a simple example. According to the theory of the phlogistians (for that is the cumbersome name we call someone who believes in phlogiston), when a candle burned it gave off phlogiston. If a glass was put over a candle, the candle soon snuffed out. Why? Because (they said) the candle finally gave off so much phlogiston that the air in the glass could hold no more. It was saturated with phlogiston! Since the air could hold no more phlogiston, the candle could burn no longer.

Now one day—and we know the day, August 1, 1774—Priestley put calx of mercury underneath a glass. He focused the sun's hot rays on the calx with his new 12" diameter magnifying glass. It began to give off a gas. The calx of mercury changed back into mercury, and Priestley trapped the gas with his pneumatic trough.

And then he sat and looked, and thought, and looked some more. He happened to have a lighted candle nearby. Without really thinking about it Priestley exposed the candle to the gas. The flame suddenly flared into brilliance! What was this wondrous gas?

If it gave such life to a flame, how would it affect living creatures? Priestley decided to test it with two mice. He put one mouse under one glass with ordinary air, and the other mouse in another glass with this new and magic air. The first mouse died in fifteen minutes. But the second mouse lived twice that long.

Mr. Priestley could not resist. He had to try some for himself. He found it quite invigorating! "My breath felt peculiarly light and easy for some time afterward," he later recalled. So far, "only my mice and myself have had the privilege of breathing it." He wondered if this air might be used by others for medicinal purposes—but also worried about a possible danger. "For as a candle burns out much faster in this air than in common air, so we might *live out too fast*. A moralist at least may say that the air which nature has provided for us is as good as we deserve."

But Priestley had to tell the world about this wonderful dephlogisticated air. Dephlogisticated?

Yes. Remember, for the phlogistians, a burning candle placed under a glass continually emitted phlogiston until the air in the glass was completely saturated. So, reasoned Priestly, if the candle burns even more brightly, then the air must not have any phlogiston at all. It must be dephlogisticated!

What really happened? He got it exactly backwards.

Calx of mercury is actually mercuric oxide. Just as with zinc, or nearly any metal, mercury picks up oxygen when it is burned in the air. That is how the mercuric oxide was produced. When Priestley burned it again with the magnifying glass, the oxygen was given off, and ran into the collecting tube.

Oxygen allows for combustion, that is, for burning. The lit candle in the covered glass goes out because it gradually burns all of the oxygen up. When there is more oxygen present than in normal air, combustion (burning) is even more vigorous.

Animals also need oxygen. The mouse in the first covered glass had used up all the oxygen in ordinary air in fifteen minutes, but the second mouse had a much larger supply—he had pure oxygen. (Normal air is only about 20% oxygen.)

So, Priestley got it exactly backwards. The air he thought was full of phlogiston was actually emptied of oxygen. The air he thought was entirely emptied of phlogiston, was actually full of oxygen.

But even though Priestley was wrong about what he found, a clearly defined error, as we said above, is sometimes the only way to the truth.

Before we see how things were put right, we need to examine another clearly defined but erroneous discovery, the discovery of hydrogen. For this we must turn to another Englishman, Mr. Henry Cavendish.

9. Mr. Cavendish and Inflammable Air

Unlike Priestley, Mr. Cavendish (1731-1810) was quite rich. You would not know it if you saw him. He always wore the same tattered and stained clothes, and unfashionably old hat. He never had time for the trifles of fine clothes and fashion. Mr. Cavendish was utterly absorbed in chemistry.

He performed many careful and important experiments, but we remember him for first identifying hydrogen, and showing that water is made up of hydrogen and oxygen—although *he* would have said

54

that water is made up of inflammable air (which he thought might be phlogiston) and dephlogisticated air.

HENRY CAVENDISH

In a famous experiment, Cavendish poured what we now know to be dilute sulfuric acid (H_2SO_4), first on zinc, then on iron, and finally on tin. Using the same method as Priestley, he trapped the gas emitted each time. Then he did the same thing again, this time pouring spirit of salt (or hydrochloric acid, HCl, as we now call it) on the three metals. And again, he carefully trapped the gas emitted each time. He touched a lit taper to each of the six samples of gas, and all burned with the same pale blue flame. It was the very same gas! Since this gas could be lit, he called it "inflammable gas," that is, gas which is able to burn.

He thought this inflammable gas came from the metals, zinc, iron, and tin, and since it burned he wondered if he might have released the phlogiston trapped in the metals! (Remember, the phlogistians thought that when metal was heated, it released phlogiston, so Cavendish reasoned that this gas might be the phlogiston contained in the metal. But he was not quite sure, and generally called the gas, "inflammable air.")

What actually happened? If we look at the chemical formulac above, H_2SO_4 and HCl, we can see. To use two examples that shall make it clear for all six, when dilute sulfuric acid was poured on iron, the iron "traded" places with the hydrogen, and the hydrogen was thereby released. If we look at our modern symbolic representation of the reaction, it will be quite clear.

$$Fe \quad + \quad H_2SO_4 \quad => \quad FeSO_4 \quad + \quad H_2$$
$$\text{(Iron)} \qquad \text{(Sulfuric Acid)} \quad \text{(Iron Sulfate)} \quad \text{(Hydrogen)}$$

Hydrochloric acid poured on iron released hydrogen in the same way. This time the iron switched places with the hydrogen to make iron chloride and hydrogen.

$$Fe \quad + \quad 2HC \quad => \quad FeCl_2 \quad + \quad H_2$$
$$\text{(Iron)} \quad \text{(Hydrochloric Acid)} \quad \text{(Iron Chloride)} \quad \text{(Hydrogen)}$$

We can see, then, that what Cavendish thought might be phlogiston was actually hydrogen. Yet, even with this confusion, it was an amazing and important discovery.

But he did something else even more amazing and important. He put dephlogisticated air (oxygen) and phlogiston or inflammable air (hydrogen) into a glass globe and sparked it with an electric current. It exploded and he found . . .

Water! Water formed on the inside of the glass globe. Oddly enough, others had done this same experiment, but it did not strike them that two gases could make water.

But they do. And furthermore, Cavendish found that if *two* volumes of inflammable air (hydrogen) were sparked with *one* volume of deplogisticated air (oxygen), all of both gases turned into water.

This was an amazing discovery—much, much more amazing than Cavendish, Priestley, or anyone else could have known at the time. *Two* volumes of hydrogen combine with *one* volume of oxygen to make a very much smaller amount of water. Cavendish had discovered the very famous chemical formula for water: H_2O . . . almost.

You see, Mr. Cavendish saw the whole thing as a phlogistian. He thought that inflammable air (hydrogen) was actually *water plus phlogiston*, and that dephlogisticated air (oxygen) was actually *water minus phlogiston*. What happens when you add water-plus-phlogiston to water-minus-phlogiston? The plus and minus phlogistons "cancel" each other out, and you are left with only water!

(water + phlogiston)   +   (water – phlogiston) = water

You see, Mr. Cavendish was still thinking of water as an element, and it wasn't until someone realized that water was actually made of two distinct gases, that the notion that water was an element could finally be rejected.

Both Priestley and Cavendish knew someone, a Frenchman who insisted that there was no such thing as phlogiston, and hence no such thing as dephlogisticated air. This French scientist invented the very names "hydrogen" and "oxygen." He argued that Priestley and Cavendish, brilliant as they were, had gotten things exactly backwards, and set out to make it right. That Frenchman's name was Antoine Lauren Lavoisier [luh VWAH zee aye].

Priestley would not listen. To his dying day, when most chemists followed Lavoisier, he was still holding fast to the nearly-dead theory of phlogiston. "I feel perfectly confident of the ground I stand upon," he declared, "truth will in time prevail over any error." Cavendish simply shrugged his shoulders, and remained a luke-warm believer in phlogiston.

Truth did prevail, but it was Lavoisier who was right, as we shall soon see.

10. Chemistry's French Revolution

Antoine Laurent Lavoisier (1743-1794) was a scientific revolutionary born in the midst of a political revolution. He found both his country and chemistry in a state of confusion, and both in serious need of reorganization and repair, and he worked with great diligence and intelligence to help both France and science. Sadly, the revolution in France cut short the life of this great revolutionary of science. But before he climbed the scaffold to the guillotine on the 8th of May in 1794, he had already completely

redefined chemistry, turning the backwards front-
wards and putting the upside-down right-side up.

Lavoisier was the son of a rich lawyer, and a de-
fender of the king of France. But things were bad in
France in the last half of the 1700s. The poor paid
too many taxes and had too little food. The rich
seemed not to care about the sad lives of the far
more numerous poor. Louis XVI, the king of
France, was neither a strong enough nor clever
enough leader to avoid the coming thunderstorm of
revolution.

ANTOINE LAVOISIER

In 1789 that storm broke, and
the entire order of France was
turned upside down. The French
Revolution had begun. But that
very same year, Lavoisier published his *Elementary Treatise on
Chemistry*, and that turned the
science of chemistry right side up.

Lavoisier did not begin as a chemist, however. He
first studied to be a lawyer, just like his father. But
someone persuaded him to sit in on a very popular
chemistry course, and young Lavoisier never thought
of being a lawyer again.

He very soon decided that he wanted to become a
member of the prestigious French Academy of Sciences, and once Lavoisier decided something, it was
already half-way to being accomplished.

When he was just over twenty years old, he en-
tered a competition sponsored by the Academy of

Sciences. "Find an economical way to light the streets of Paris," they commanded the competitors. Lavoisier spent long hard hours on the problem. For his suggestions, King Louis the XV ordered that young Lavoisier be given a gold medal.

All his life he did many things for his country and her kings. He found French gunpowder to be the most poorly made in Europe. Under his direction it became the best. He tried to bring about a better supply of water to Paris, and advocated the use of fire hydrants as well. He called for reforms of the prisons, and for the government to pay for life insurance for the poor. He tried to help the farmers by showing them better methods of cultivating their land. He did all these things and more for his beloved France.

But his greatest achievement was the reform of chemistry, something he did not only for France, but for the whole world.

Some historians of science think that Lavoisier did not discover anything new. They argue that he merely took the pieces of the chemical puzzle that various scientists had already been puzzling over, and showed them how they really fit. Others think that Lavoisier did indeed discover many, very important things. Who is right? Well, it's difficult to say. Read on, and see what *you* think!

Everyone agrees that Lavoisier was the first to see that the phlogistians had everything backwards. In October of 1774 he happened to meet Mr. Priestley in Paris. At dinner Priestley described his creation of dephlogisticated air by heating calx of mercury. Lavoisier sat wide-eyed, and drank in everything Priestley said about this strange pure air that made candles dazzlingly bright. He had to repeat these experiments in his own laboratory—immediately.

He returned to his laboratory, cooked and measured, and scratched his head. He heated and boiled and weighed, and paced up and down. Something was very right with Mr. Priestley's experiment, but very wrong in Mr. Priestley's interpretation.

And then, *voilà*, it all fell into place.

Voilà is French for "behold!" or "see there!" Lavoisier set up an experiment to *see* whether his suspicions were correct. He suspected that the air, or something in the air, was going *into* the mercury, and making the calx.

Lavoisier put 4 ounces of mercury into a glass retort, a French version of the alembic. Lavoisier's retort had a very long neck that stretched up from the vessel bulb, then down and back up again like a letter "J." The hook of the "J" went under another glass jar shaped like a bell. This bell jar was to be used like Mr. Priestley's pneumatic trough, but with two very important differences. First, instead of trapping gas in the bell jar, Lavoisier was trying to see if air was *removed from* the bell jar, drawn back up the "J" tube, and into the mercury. Second, to measure *how much* air was removed, Lavoisier did not fill the bell jar full of liquid—he used mercury—but filled it with just enough mercury so that 50 cubic inches of air would remain in the bell jar when turned upside down in a tank of mercury. Here is Lavoisier's device.

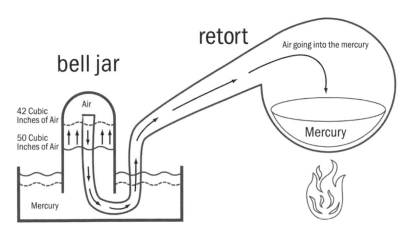

Lavoisier proves that air goes *into* heated mercury because the air in the bell jar shrinks from 50 cubic inches to 42 cubic inches.

Lavoisier went to work. He heated the mercury for one day. Nothing happened. But the second day red specks started to appear on the mercury. Calx of mercury! He heated and heated for a total of twelve days until no more red specks appeared.

The air in the container? It had *contracted* from 50 cubic inches to 42 cubic inches. "See there!" he cried.

Lavoisier had proven that the phlogistians had it backwards. They said that when a metal like mercury was heated, phlogiston flew *out* of it. But Lavoisier had shown that, on the contrary, air had gone *into* it. Eight cubic inches of air, to be exact!

And that, Lavoisier concluded, was why the metal *gained* weight when it was heated. (Not because phlogiston weighed less than zero!)

But what *kind* of air was it? Was it air, or something *in* the air? Lavoisier had to know.

He gathered the red specks that had formed on the mercury, and heated them strongly, gathering the gas that they gave off.

What was it? Priestley's dephlogisticated air! Eight cubic inches of it!

But contrary to Priestley and the phlogistians, Lavoisier had just shown that heated metal did not give off phlogiston. Instead, it gained a gas from the air. Neither phlogiston nor dephlogisticated air were real. The dephlogisticated air must be something else. Lavoisier named it oxygen (from the Greek words meaning acid-generator, because Lavoisier thought all acids included oxygen).

Lavoisier now re-explained everything the right way.

When a candle burning under a glass jar snuffed out, it was not because the candle had finally filled the air in the jar with phlogiston, but because the candle had used up all the oxygen from the air.

When a mouse put under a glass jar soon died, Lavoisier argued, that was simply because the mouse, like the candle, needed oxygen.

Indeed, argued Lavoisier, combustion (burning) and respiration (breathing) both required oxygen because respiration is a kind of combustion. Animal bodies need oxygen to burn the food, and create heat for their bodies.

But Lavoisier's revolution had just begun. He now turned to Cavendish's experiments which were supposed to prove that inflammable air and dephlogisticated air produce water, and set these aright too.

He put together some oxygen (dephlogisticated air) and some of Cavendish's inflammable air, and sparked them. Water, just as Cavendish had reported. But Cavendish had thought that inflammable air was actually water plus phlogiston. "Nonsense," replied Lavoisier. "Phlogiston does not exist. Inflammable air must be an element itself."

Lavoisier named it hydrogen, which comes from the Greek words meaning water-generator.

And so, after centuries and centuries, going all the way back to Thales, Lavoisier had finally seen clearly that water was not an element at all, but was made out of two elements, two more fundamental things, oxygen and hydrogen.

And the air? It was not an element either, but made of (at least) two elements.

Remember the 50 cubic inches of air in the first experiment? Lavoisier had shown that there were 8 cubic inches of oxygen in it. That meant, argued Lavoisier, that common air, which everyone had thought was an element, was made up of about 16% oxygen. (Later, Lavoisier calculated it at about 20% oxygen, which is closer to the real figure of 20.948%.)

What kind of gas was the 42 cubic inches left over?

Lavoisier tested it. A candle would not burn in it. A mouse would not live in it. He called it azote, which means no-life. A bit later, a man named Jean Chaptal gave it the name we call it today, nitrogen. But whether it was called azote or nitrogen, the important thing was that Lavoisier identified it as an element that makes up air.

Interestingly enough, Lavoisier is often not credited with the discovery of nitrogen. Instead, the credit is given to Daniel Rutherford (1749-1819). While it is true that Mr. Rutherford was the first to isolate nitrogen—although we must add that Priestley and Cavendish had also done so about the same time—Rutherford did not identify it correctly. He thought it was air saturated with phlogiston!

But, as we have seen, Lavoisier proved that phlogiston did not exist. Mr. Lavoisier and his wife Marie were so confident and so excited by Lavoisier's proofs that they staged a celebration, where Marie, acting as a priestess, burned the writings of phlogiston's first proponents, Becher and Stahl, on an altar!

Lavoisier was, we imagine, sure to point out that the burning paper was using oxygen, and not giving off phlogiston—unless we consider the burning of the theory the final sending off of phlogiston!

But he was still not finished with his revolution.

Lavoisier was the first to make clear a very important principle in chemistry, one which is used in the above experiments. It has come to be called the *conservation of mass.* It is a very simple but very profound principle, for it allows chemistry to keep a balance sheet.

"One may take it for granted," Lavoisier pronounced grandly, "that in every reaction there is an equal quantity of matter before and after the operation."

If the 50 cubic inches of air in which mercury is heated drops down to 42 inches, then the 8 cubic inches of oxygen must still be somewhere. It does not disappear but changes places. It is no longer in the air, but in the mercury. The mercury has gained the 8 cubic inches—not in size, but in weight—and weighs as much as the original mercury plus 8 cubic inches of oxygen. There is still the same amount of matter. It is just in a different form.

It is easy to see how revolutionary were Lavoisier's contributions. But even with all these wonderful things, Lavoisier had yet other changes in mind.

11. A Revolution in Names

This revolution needed a new system of names, thought Lavoisier, names which reflected the elements of which things are actually made. Calx of mercury is really mercury that has taken on oxygen, and so it should be called mercuric oxide. That is how we still name chemical compounds today.

If you read a textbook of chemistry written prior to the publication of Lavoisier's *Elementary Treatise on Chemistry*, it would make no sense because it would use such names as had been used all the way back to the days of alchemy—powder of Algaroth, turbith mineral, colcothar, phagadenic water, pomphlix, Glauber's salt, oil of vitriol, butter of arsenic, sugar of lead, and liver of sulphur. But a modern chemistry student who picks up Lavoisier's *Elementary Treatise on Chemistry*, would feel right at home, for it is the home which Lavoisier himself designed, and almost all of the names of the chemical elements and compounds would be familiar.

You would not find 109 elements, however, but only 33. Most of these 33 would be the elements on our own chart today, but some are no longer counted as elements.

You would find 6 non-metals: sulfur, phosphorous, charcoal, muriatic radical, flouric radical, and boracic radical.

But only sulfur and phosphorous remain on our element chart today (although one might consider charcoal to be close enough to carbon).

You would find 17 metals: antimony, arsenic, bismuth, cobalt, copper, gold, iron, lead, manganese, mercury, molybdenum, nickel, platinum, silver, tin, tungsten, and zinc. All of these will still be found on our Periodic Table of Elements.

You would find five of what he called simple earths: lime, magnesia, barytes, alumina, and silica. You will not find any of these on the Periodic Table, however, because they are not simple at all. Lavoisier was wrong. They are not elements but compounds. The real elements aluminum and silicon were not isolated and properly identified until the first quarter of the 19th century. Lime is a compound of calcium and oxygen; magnesia is a compound of magnesium, carbon, and oxygen; barytes is composed, for the most part, of barium, sulfur, and oxygen.

And finally, you would find the following five elements: Light, Caloric, Oxygen, Azote, and Hydrogen. Three of these five will be found today (with azote's renaming as nitrogen).

Light and Caloric? Lavoisier thought that Light and Caloric (that is, heat) were elements. Fortunately, this error did not disturb the soundness of the foundations of chemistry he was building.

But Lavoisier gave us a way to fix even his own mistakes by establishing a proper definition of what an element is. *An element is the last point which chemical analysis is capable of reaching.* If it cannot be taken apart by any further chemical analysis, it is an element; if it can, it is not an element but a chemical compound. Water is not an element, but oxygen and hydrogen are.

This definition allowed Lavoisier to do away with the old list of four elements, earth, water, air, and fire, and build a new list consisting of those substances which he thought could not be broken down any further.

But . . . he thought scientists had to keep testing the items on the list, and keep looking for new elements. And they did. As we have seen, some of the elements Lavoisier listed were actually compounds.

Many new elements were added. And finally, some, like Light and Caloric, were found not to be either elements or compounds.

There is one last thing we must notice about Lavoisier's list of elements. They are not yet put in the *place* that we find them on the Periodic Table. They are just in a list.

The elements could not be shuffled around into their right places until other revolutionaries completed what Lavoisier had begun.

Who knows—Lavoisier might have done it himself. But another revolution, the French Revolution, cut his days short.

Although Lavoisier had done many things to help both the rich and the poor in France, before and after 1789, the political revolutionaries believed that anyone who had helped the King at all was an enemy of the people—even if he had helped the people too!

On the 24th of November he was arrested in his laboratory in the midst of an experiment. He was tried by the revolutionary court, and his "guilt" was quickly established.

The charges? Mr. Lavoisier was guilty of adding water to tobacco, of building a wall around Paris to the detriment of the people's health, and of collecting excess taxes—all of these charges being merely trumped up so that Lavoisier could be executed by his enemies.

On May 8, 1794 Lavoisier walked up the steps to the guillotine. The great French mathematician Joseph Louis Lagrange sadly remarked, "It required only a moment to sever his head, and probably one hundred years will not suffice to produce another like it."

12. "Nature Never Creates Other Than Balance in Hand"

It may have looked, with Lavoisier, that all the hard work of chemistry had been done. While Lavoisier certainly set things going in the right direction, there was still much to be discovered on the way to the Periodic Table. Nature seems always to have more surprises, and the more we look into its order, the more order we find.

But now we have to move from the visible to the invisible world, from the macroscopic to the microscopic. We must move, in short, to the atomic world, for it is there that we shall find the logic of the Periodic Table's delightful order.

Now it is true that Lavoisier gave chemistry a very sound, if humble, definition of an element—"the last point which analysis is capable of reaching." But what happens, we might wonder, when we dig more deeply, down beyond the level of the visible elements like silver, gold, and sulfur? Are each of these made of smaller pieces of silver, gold, and sulfur, or something else?

That is just the kind of question chemists were asking each other around the beginning of the 19th century, just after the time of Lavoisier. And to answer it, chemistry had to reach back to Boyle and his atoms. But this did not happen all at once. Chemists were very cautious folk. They did not go in for airy speculation about things they could not see. They wanted solid reasons based on the evidence of what was right before their eyes in the laboratory.

We may begin with a German chemist, Jeremias Richter [RICK ter] (1762-1807). As with many of the greatest of discoveries, Richter's contribution to science was the result, not of doing anything new, but of looking more carefully at what had already been done.

Chemists (and indeed, alchemists) had been working with acids and bases for a long, long time—centuries. They knew that bases neutralized acids and acids neutralized bases.

You most probably realized the same thing when you were pouring baking soda (the base) into the vinegar (the acid). You kept pouring in baking soda until it would not fizz anymore. At the point, just where it first stopped fizzing, the solution was neutralized (unless you poured too much baking soda in, in which case you made the solution a base).

If you thought to test it with the purple cabbage juice, you would find that the juice stayed purple, and that was a sign that it was neither an acid any longer (for that turns the juice red), nor had it yet gone over to become a base (thereby turning the juice green). This solution between the acid and the base chemists at the time called a "salt," but today we say that it has a pH of 7 on a scale that runs from 0 (strongest acid) to 14 (strongest base).

You may then have wondered *how much* of a base it takes to neutralize a certain amount of acid. If you did, and you wanted to know the same thing in regard to other acids and other bases, then congratulations, you were thinking just like Richter.

Richter asked himself, "If I take 1000 parts of sulfuric acid (a "part" just means any amount you happen to choose, whether a gallon or a teaspoon), how much of each base that I know will it take to neutralize it?" Fairly soon, after a lot of careful measuring, he drew up a table of comparison. (A man named Ernst Fischer reorganized Richter's table in a clearer way, so we will use his, and even then, only some of the table.)

Bases	Parts	Acids	Parts
Magnesia	615	Sulfuric Acid	1000
Ammonia	672	Phosphoric Acid	979
Soda	859	Nitric Acid	1405
Potash	1605	Citric Acid	1583

How does Richter's table work?

Quite ingeniously!

If you want to neutralize 1000 parts of sulfuric acid, you simply use 615 parts of Magnesia *or* 672 parts of Ammonia *or* 859 parts of Soda *or* 1605 parts of Potash. And what if you were out of Sulfuric acid? Well, you could just substitute 1405 parts of Nitric acid. Low on Nitric acid? Use 979 parts of Phosphoric acid instead. And so on with all the other acids and bases.

The table was called the Table of Equivalents, because it gave the equivalent amounts of bases and acids for achieving neutralization.

All very interesting, but what does it have to do with getting us to the invisible world of the atom?

Isn't it odd that the relationships are *so regular?* That wherever you are, anywhere in the world, exactly 859 parts of soda will neutralize 1583 parts of citric acid. It suggests that all these chemical compounds, both acids and bases, are very precisely formulated.

Chemical compounds, that is to say, are not like vegetable soup. You do not find that you get vegetable soup only if you combine exactly 49 parts of carrots and 87 parts of potatoes to 100 parts of water. Vegetable soup has a recipe, rather than a formula. You take a few cups of water, put in some carrots, some potatoes, a sprig of parsley, a handful of peas, and a pinch or two of your favorites spices. A recipe is a matter of more and less; but a formula is very exact.

There is another sign of exactness on Richter's chart. We only find *whole* numbers. Not just a little over 615.3728493049 parts of Magnesia, but 615 parts on the button. Very strange. Things are so neat and precise that it looked like a conspiracy of order.

But even more interesting things were soon discovered. For these, we turn to the controversy between two French chemists, Claude Berthollet [ber tow LAY] (1748-1822) and Joseph Proust [PROOST] (1754-1826).

Both Berthollet and Proust, and many other chemists besides, recognized that they could make different compounds using different amounts of the very same elements. For example, they both knew that the two elements carbon and oxygen could make two different compounds, one called carbonic oxide and the other called carbonic acid.

Now Berthollet thought that the elements of a compound could come together in variable and indefinite ways. To continue our example, if Berthollet was right, you could keep adding just a little bit more oxygen to carbon and make a whole continuous line of compounds between carbonic oxide and carbonic acid (like going from black to white through various shades of gray).

But Proust thought the exact opposite. He argued that each compound had a definite formula, so that elements combined only in very definite and invariable ways. Using our example again, if Proust was right, there were no compounds in between carbonic oxide and carbonic acid. No grays. Just black and white, so to speak.

Proust won the argument. Not by words, but by repeated experiments. If we use the names of the compounds we use today, we see that chemistry has followed Proust. Carbon dioxide (carbonic acid) will always contain exactly twice as much oxygen by weight as carbon monoxide (carbonic oxide)—the prefix "di-" means "two," and "mono-" means "one"—and there are no compounds in between.

This is called the *Law of Definite Proportions* (or sometimes it is called the Law of Constant Composition). In its precise form, the Law is stated: "In a compound, the constituent elements are always present in a definite proportion by weight."

That means that compounds are not recipes (such as we use for soup) but very precise formulae (such as we use in mathematics). We find exactly two times as much oxygen by weight, not a little over or under 1.83940364. The amount by weight of each element in different chemical compounds always changes by a whole number: 2 times as much, 3 times as much, even 4 times as much.

This becomes clearer if we look at a list of compounds made from two elements in modern symbols, along with their modern names. (The numbers here do not, we should mention, symbolize weight, except quite indirectly. But it is direct enough for our purposes.)

CH_4	methane	1 carbon atom and 4 hydrogen atoms
C_2H_4	ethene	2 carbon atoms and 4 hydrogen atoms
C_3H_6	propene	3 carbon atoms and 6 hydrogen atoms
C_3H_8	propane	3 carbon atoms and 8 hydrogen atoms

But we must note that chemists at the time did not speak of "1 carbon atom" or "8 hydrogen atoms, " nor did they have such symbols as CH_4 or C_3H_8. They only knew that the weight of each element was double or triple or quadruple. (We shall soon go to John Dalton and Jöns Berzelius to find such atoms and symbols.)

But Proust did know that elements are not just thrown together any old way to make chemical compounds. As he declared: "We must recognize an invisible hand which holds the balance in the formation of compounds. A compound is a substance to which Nature assigns fixed ratios." That is, to use again our modern notation, if the ratio of carbon to oxygen in CO is 1:1, then the ratio of carbon to oxygen in CO_2 is 1:2.

For Proust, then, a compound was something "which Nature never creates other than balance in hand." Nature works by formulae; chefs work by recipes. It is as if the designer of nature were something of a mathematician rather than a cook!

Very strange and very wonderful. Now we had better get on to the atomic world, where things are even more strange and even more wonderful.

DALTON

13. Mr. Dalton and His Atoms

Perhaps you feel that you will never get anywhere in life because you are not rich. Or you are tall and lanky like a walking vine. Or you have a very gruff voice, and even worse, people start yawning and leaving the room when you speak. Or maybe your chin and your nose are both so long and pointed that they almost touch each other. Perhaps you are color-blind. And maybe you are so busy that you cannot get your work done properly.

If you had one or two of these problems, you might consider yourself quite unfortunate. But if you had all of these problems, you would be John Dalton, one of the most famous chemists of all time, and the founder of the modern atomic theory in chemistry. So keep that in mind.

JOHN DALTON

John Dalton (1766-1844) was born in Eaglesfield, England, the son of a poor weaver. He, like his father, was a Quaker. From the time he was very young, John Dalton had to make his way in the world. He was largely self-educated, and earned his living for much of his life by teaching. In fact, he began to teach school when he was just twelve!

Perhaps Dalton's most helpful trait was his perseverance. In the "race" to make chemical discoveries, there are tortoises and there are hares, and Mr. Dalton, by his own admission, was a tortoise, a very diligent one too.

For example, he began to keep a daily journal called "Observations on the Weather" in 1787, where he wrote down everything and anything he could about the rain, the snow, the fog, the atmospheric pressure, the levels of water vapor in the air, and so on. He plodded all over England with his thermometer and barometer, up hills, down into valleys, through the bogs, and into the forests, and he did it for 57 more years. The last journal entry was made the night before he died.

That is perseverance. And such perseverance paid off, because his observations on the action of gases in the atmosphere led him to formulate his atomic theory.

Dalton learned about atoms when he studied Sir Isaac Newton's works. A little over a century before Dalton, Newton had used the "corpuscular philosophy" (as atomism was called) to explain and predict the way the planets and stars moved, as well as how the tides here on earth worked. Dalton also read Boyle, and so had heard about atoms from him. He was even familiar with those ancient atomists, Democritus, Epicurus, and Lucretius.

But none of these men had ever *seen* an atom, for if atoms existed, they were much, much too small to see. Nor had any of these men *proven* that atoms exist. Therefore, none of these men could satisfy so practical a person as Mr. John Dalton.

So while Dalton did believe that atoms existed, he wanted this belief to rest on much more solid foundations. If we look at what is old and new in Dalton's theory, we will see how he tried to build those foundations.

He supposed that all matter, all physical "stuff" however big or small, was made of solid, indestructible, indivisible atoms. (He used little wooden spheres to represent them when he taught.) But this was not new. All the atomists, ancient and modern thought that.

He assumed that there were as many different

kinds of atoms as there were elements—for him, about 50 at the time. That was new, for the previous atomists, both ancient and modern, thought that all the atoms were made of the same universal "stuff," and differed only in their sizes and shapes. But Dalton thought that there were hydrogen atoms, and oxygen atoms, and sulfur atoms, and so on down the line.

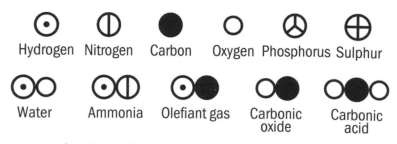

Dalton invented a symbol system to signify the different atoms and their combination in compound.

He also thought that the reason chemical combinations occurred in ratios of whole numbers by weight (the Law of Definite Proportions, given to us by Proust), was that the whole numbers ultimately stood for . . . individual atoms, of course. That was very new, and very important.

So if you said to Mr. Dalton, "Good Sir, why *is* there exactly twice as much oxygen by weight in carbonic acid as there is in carbonic oxide?" He would reply: "Very simple. Because there are twice as many oxygen atoms in carbonic acid."

This was called the *Law of Multiple Proportions, which states, in Dalton's words, "In the formation of two or more compounds from the same elements, the weights of one element that combine with a fixed weight of a second element are in a ratio of small whole numbers (integers) such as 2 to 1, 3 to 1, 3 to 2, or 4 to 3."

He even thought, from this, that he could *weigh* the atoms. That was very, very new, and a seemingly impossible dream.

Let's look more closely at these last two points.

We recall that Proust found that chemical compounds made of the same elements were ruled by very exact formulae; and he also found that they always occurred in whole number multiples.

Dalton set out to explain why the formulae were so exact. Here, we must remember that Dalton was not looking at the chemical formulae we have today, such as CH_4 or C_2H_4. (With these, you can tell very quickly that the first has one atom of carbon and four atoms of hydrogen, and the second has two carbon atoms and four hydrogen atoms.) These symbols were invented *because of* Dalton's theory. All Dalton himself had were the chemical names used at the time, such as "carbureted hydrogen" and "olefiant gas."

Dalton, like Proust, noticed that two elements could combine to form two distinct chemical compounds. For instance, Dalton noted that carbon and hydrogen could form olefiant gas, but if the hydrogen was doubled, he got something else, carbureted hydrogen.

Hmmm, thought Dalton, what does that mean?

And he wrote down this in his notebook: ● ☉ olefiant gas

And then this: ☉ ● ☉ carbureted hydrogen

The blackened dot ● was Dalton's symbol for a carbon atom. The white circle with a dot ☉ was Dalton's symbol for a hydrogen atom. When he put them next to each other it meant that the atoms were linked as elements in a compound. So a big glass jar full of the compound "carbureted hydrogen" was, so Dalton said, made up of thousands, or maybe millions, of ☉ ● ☉'s, and there were twice as many ☉'s in that glass jar, as there would be if the same jar were filled with an equal amount of ● ☉'s. If you don't believe him, well just count for yourself:

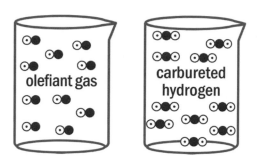

That was an enormous leap forward for chemistry—even if it was a leap of faith, for he still had not seen an atom. But the leap explained why chemical combinations were so very regular. Different compounds made of the same elements differed by the number of atoms. Each atom, we might say, stands for a whole number. That is why today, for example, we write CH_4 for methane and C_2H_4 for ethene.

But—forgive us for pointing this out, Mr. Dalton—in getting things right in one way, Dalton managed to get them wrong in another. Olefiant gas is today called "ethene" and carbureted hydrogen is now called "methane."

What's wrong? Dalton thought that carbureted hydrogen (methane, CH_4) had twice as much hydrogen as olefiant gas (ethene, C_2H_4). But if you look at our modern formulae, you can see that they both have the exact same amount of hydrogen atoms: four. The truth of the matter, was that olefiant gas (ethene) had *twice* the carbon, not half the hydrogen.

Even more important, he had the *total* number of atoms in each compound wrong. Olefiant gas (ethene, C_2H_4) actually has two carbon atoms and four hydrogen atoms, not (as Dalton thought) one carbon and one hydrogen atom. And carbureted hydrogen (methane, CH_4) has one carbon atom and four hydrogen atoms, not (as Dalton thought) one carbon and two hydrogen atoms.

So we might say that Dalton got it right but in the wrong way, or he got it wrong but in the right way. In either case, however, even if he did not get the compounds exactly right all the time, Dalton's general ideas of atomism led chemistry toward thinking of the elements in terms of distinct atoms—which is how they appear on the Periodic Table and in our chemical formulae.

Even so, we should ask what caused Dalton to get the wrong number of atoms in each case? As we shall see in the next chapter, the error lay in trying to determine the number of atoms by the *weight* of each of the separate elements in the compound.

Having said this, however, we must not leap to the conclusion that using weight was a bad idea, an idea which could only lead to error. In fact, it was a very good idea, and (ironically) led to the correction of the problem of using weight! Sometimes the only way out of the forest is a winding path. Let's follow that important path right now.

Atoms, Dalton thought, must have weight. But how, how could he possibly weigh them?

Atomic weight
on our Periodic
Table today

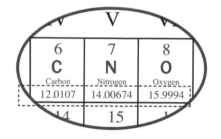

He knew he could not put these tiniest of things on a scale, but he thought he could figure out their *relative* weight. And even if the relative weights of the atoms have not turned out exactly as Dalton had calculated them, still, if we look at our Periodic Table, we see "Atomic Weight." So, if Dalton had not tried to "weigh" the atom—at least indirectly—we never would have gotten to the Periodic Table.

So how did he do it? And what is *relative* weight?

Well, pretend that you had a big box of the smallest possible black and white marbles, too small and too many either to weigh or to count one by one. All that you knew, was that for every white marble there was one black marble.

You also had a magic marble sorter, which could put all the white marbles in one bucket and all the black marbles in another. If the marbles are, as we said, too many and too small to weigh and count directly, could you do it indirectly?

Yes, you could. Suppose the bucket of white marbles weighed 10 pounds and the bucket of black marbles weighed 20 pounds. Since you know that there are exactly the same number of white marbles

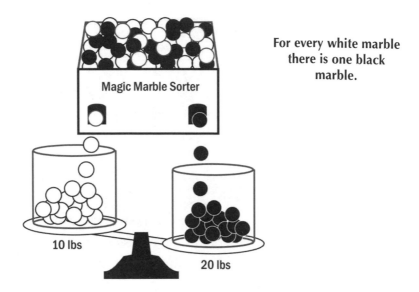

For every white marble there is one black marble.

Magic Marble Sorter

10 lbs

20 lbs

as black marbles, you know that each of the black marbles must weigh twice as much as each of the white marbles.

You do not know how much a white marble itself weighs, but you know the weight of the black marble *relative to* the white marble. That is an example of relative weight.

Dalton reasoned the very same way with atoms. We'll use his symbols. If we know that the atomic formula of water is ⊙O, and we have a certain amount of it in a jar, then we can separate all the ⊙s from the O's, and weigh each. Now, as we have seen above, Dalton used ⊙ to symbolize hydrogen, and hydrogen was the lightest element, so Dalton weighed everything relative to hydrogen. (He used hydrogen in the same way—or the same weigh!—as we used the white marble above.) The other symbol

O was his symbol for oxygen.

So the calculation of the relative weights of oxygen and hydrogen are fairly simple. Dalton used the best measurement for the amount of hydrogen and oxygen in water available at the time. According to Lavoisier, water was 15% hydrogen and 85% oxygen by weight. That is, in each ⊙ O, the ⊙ atom made up 15% of the entire weight, and the O atom made up 85%. And so Dalton simply divided 85 by 15, and declared that an oxygen atom weighed 5.5 times as much as a hydrogen atom! Later Dalton used the more accurate figures of another chemist, Joseph Gay-Lussac [gay lew SAHK], who determined that water was 12.6 parts hydrogen and 87.4 parts oxygen by weight, and so Dalton got the relative weight as 6.94, which he rounded up to 7.

Then, he proceeded to weigh other compounds, and determine the weight of other elements in relation to hydrogen, and he kept figuring and refiguring these atomic weights the rest of his life.

Brilliant!

But—forgive us again, Mr. Dalton—even though it was the right idea, it was not very accurate. Chemists soon found out that water was made of two hydrogen atoms and not one, and found ways to measure far more accurately. The calculations of Mr. Dalton, then, are not used any longer. But again, his *ideas* about the way to measure led, ultimately, to the atomic weights you see on the Periodic Table.

Finally, we note that Mr. Dalton's symbols are no

longer with us either. Not many chemists used his dot symbols, but the idea of using symbols to represent the *atoms* of an element (rather than just using a general name for the element) stayed with us. Such symbols allow chemists to represent all kinds of complex chemical reactions and formulae in a very compact, short-hand way.

It was a man named Jöns Jakob Berzelius [ber SAY lee oos] (1779-1848) who got the idea of representing atoms by letters. It was he who gave us O for oxygen, C for carbon, Co for cobalt, S for sulfur, and so on. But even though Berzelius told chemists in 1813 that this was the best way to symbolize the chemicals, it took about fifty years for chemists to accept his letter symbols and use them regularly. But they are (with a few exceptions) the symbols we use today.

Dalton did not like Berzelius' letter symbols, however. Not in the least. In fact, he hated them! "Berzelius' symbols are horrifying," he steamed. That same year, he became so angry while discussing Berzelius' symbols with a visitor that he had a stroke!

Berzelius' symbols won out anyway. And despite this disagreement, if we take the accomplishments of Dalton and Berzelius together, we are much, much closer to having our modern Periodic Table. But being closer, is different from having arrived. So on we go to the next step.

HUMPHREY DAVY

14. The Shocking Mr. Davy

We said in the last chapter that in the race to make chemical discoveries, there are tortoises and hares. Mr. Dalton was a tortoise. Now we shall meet a hare, the dashing and rather shocking Sir Humphry Davy (1778-1829), a native of Cornwall, England.

Like Dalton, Davy was poor—the son of a poor farmer who could have been rich if only a wealthy uncle had not left his will unsigned. So Davy's father stayed poor, and so did young Humphry.

But young Humphry would not be satisfied with the life of a near-penniless farmer. He became apprenticed to a Mr. John Borlase, a surgeon and apothecary. But Mr. Davy would not become a doctor, for a copy of Lavoisier's *Elements of Chemistry* fell into his hands. Soon enough, Davy was discharged from Mr. Borlase's service because of his habit of performing explosive experiments.

After his dismissal, Davy met Mr. Thomas Beddoes, who was convinced that the various kinds of gases that had recently been discovered or created might be of some medical benefit. Beddoes founded the Pneumatic Institute, and convinced Davy to be his assistant.

HUMPHREY DAVY

Davy's daring, even foolhardy, disregard for his own safety in his quest for chemical knowledge nearly ended in his early demise. He performed all kinds of quite dangerous experiments for the Institute, inhaling a great variety of gases, some of which almost caused his suffocation. His most famous discovery, or at least the discovery that first brought him fame, was that the inhalation of nitrous oxide had rather strange effects. "A thrilling, extending from the chest to the extremities, was almost immediately produced," reported Davy. The more popular name of nitrous oxide? Laughing gas.

Unlike Mr. Priestley, who thought inhaling pure oxygen might tempt people to "live out" their lives "too fast," Mr. Davy was only too happy to promote the use of nitrous oxide merely for its strange physical effects. Soon, he was quite famous.

But more serious things than laughing gas lay ahead for Davy. The very same year, 1800, that he published his researches on nitrous oxide, an Italian physicist, Alessandro Volta (1745-1827) published a paper describing the production of a continuous electrical current from a *pile* of alternating silver and zinc discs separated by blotting paper soaked in salt water. The larger the pile, the stronger the current.

Now these great *voltaic piles* of alternating metals (or batteries, as they came to be called), were found to have a very curious effect on chemical compounds, an effect which would not only lead to the discovery of more elements, but to the very inner secrets governing the entire order of the Periodic Table of Elements. The electric current decomposed chemical compounds.

It was soon found that when the electrical current, running from the pile through wires, was applied to water, the water was decomposed into hydrogen and oxygen—and the hydrogen went to the negative pole and the oxygen went to the positive pole!

Davy applied the voltaic pile to various minerals and found that the current decomposed these minerals into alkalis (or bases) and acids, the alkalis clinging to the negative poles and the acids to the positive poles.

Perhaps, thought Davy, we can "shock" apart the alkalis themselves, especially the ones that had resisted all attempts by chemists to break them down further. He seized the voltaic piles and used them like battering rams to break down these stubborn alkalis.

First potash, which many thought was itself an element. Davy hooked the voltaic pile to moistened caustic potash. Very soon, Davy tells us, "small globules having a high metallic luster" similar to mercury appeared at the negative pole. He could not contain his joy. As his cousin and assistant later reported, "he actually danced about the room in ecstatic delight; some little time was required for him to compose himself to continue the experiment."

And he called this new metallic element *potassium* (K).

Two days later, he was able to decompose caustic soda, another alkali, and discovered another metallic element, which he named *sodium* (Na).

The next year he charged at magnesia, lime (or calx), strontites, and barytes, and discovered further metallic elements, which he named magnesium (Mg), calcium (Ca), strontium (Sr), and barium (Ba).

Davy also used the voltaic pile to prove that muriatic acid, which Lavoisier thought to be some kind of an acid formed with oxygen, was actually an element. He did it by showing that, no matter how hard he tried, he could not break down muriatic acid with an electric current. He declared it to be an element, and named it *chlorine* (Cl).

Certainly discovering all these elements was a grand thing, but an even grander discovery was in store. The effects of electricity on compounds made Davy suspect that, since an electric current broke down chemical bonds, that the chemical bonds themselves must somehow be electrical in nature. If electrolysis (that is, the use of an electric current to decompose a compound) caused elements and compounds to be attracted either to the negative or positive poles, then, thought Davy, the elements *themselves* must somehow be electrically positive and negative.

It would take over a hundred years to see how absolutely marvelous Davy's suspicion was. As we shall see, the nature of the elements themselves and their positions in the Periodic Table are both the results of these mysterious electrical charges.

But we must be patient. As wonderful as Mr. Davy's discoveries were, there were brambles of confusion that had to be cleared away before chemistry could advance further. So into the thicket we go.

JOSEPH LOUIS
GAY-LUSSAC

AVOGADRO

15. Gay-Lussac and Avagadro to the Rescue!

Now we must return to Mr. Dalton. Just when things seemed to be clearing up, they got muddled again. We recall that John Dalton was certainly on the right track, but that in getting the right way of going about things—establishing relative atomic weights—he got entangled in errors not only about the weights themselves but about the number of atoms in what he was attempting to weigh.

As is the way with most things, the one error made the other worse. During the early part of the 19th century, the time of Dalton, the weighing of elements in compounds was simply not very accurate. And if there are inaccuracies made in the relative weight of an element—oxygen, for example—then those mistakes will carry over into all the other calculations that depend on the first. That is exactly what happened.

For example, if (as Dalton did) we miscalculate the relative weight of oxygen in water (which consists of hydrogen and oxygen) as 7, and then use *that* weight to calculate the weight of carbon in carbonic acid (which consists of carbon and oxygen), then the mistake with the oxygen carries over into the relative weight of carbon. Just as with arithmetic, the miscalculations run like falling dominoes through all the other calculations.

A significant part of the inaccuracy in calculating relative weight was caused by another, more serious problem. If you make a mistake like Dalton's about the *number* of atoms in a compound, then that mistake will run through all the other calculations as well. It will only make the inaccuracies in weighing the elements in compounds all the worse!

For example, because Dalton thought that water was made up of *one* atom of hydrogen and *one* atom of oxygen, he miscalculated the relative weight of oxygen. For water, as we now know, is made up of *two* hydrogen atoms, not one.

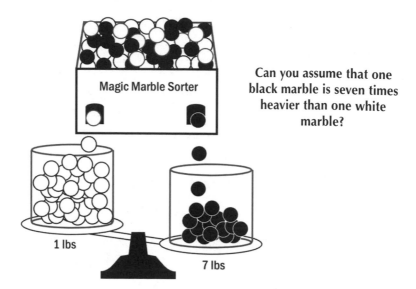

Can you assume that one black marble is seven times heavier than one white marble?

To understand Mr. Dalton's error, let's return to the magic marble sorter that helped us understand how relative atomic weight was calculated. Remember that the black and white marbles are too small either to see or to weigh individually. Now suppose that the sorter sorts the black and white marbles with the following result: the bucket of white marbles weighs 1 pound and the bucket of black marbles weighs 7 pounds.

Could you conclude that the weight of a black marble relative to the weight of a white marble was 7?

The answer is no. Why not?

You cannot assume that there are the *same* number of marbles in each bucket. Remember, they are too small to see.

If there really were 100 white marbles in the one bucket and 100 black marbles in the other, then you could conclude that the weight of the black marble relative to the weight of the white marble was 7.

But what if you found out that there are actually 200 white marbles in the one bucket and 100 black marbles in the other? *Then* what is the relative weight of the black marble?

The white marbles actually weigh $1/2$ of what you had originally thought, which is the same as saying that the black marbles weigh *twice* as much. So, instead of the relative weight of the black marble being 7, it should actually be 14.

To return to the example of water, Dalton's error lay in *assuming* that there was only 1 hydrogen atom in water. Since, as we now know, there are really 2, then an individual hydrogen atom actually weighs $1/2$ of what Dalton had thought, which is the same as saying that the oxygen atom is twice as heavy—with a relative weight of 14, not 7! Now a relative weight of 14 for oxygen is much, much closer to the relative weight 15.9994 of oxygen we use today.

But we are looking ahead. At the time, none of this was clear. So both problems had to be fixed—by better weighing techniques and by an accurate grasp of the number of atoms of each element in a compound. It took about fifty years to sort it all out. During that time, chemists used all kinds of weights for the elements, and could not agree on the number of atoms in compounds. Things got so confused, that chemists had a great deal of trouble talking to each other.

The man who first helped to sort things out was Joseph Louis Gay-Lussac (1778-1850), a Frenchman. In fact, Monsieur Gay-Lussac published the paper that would help to clear things up in 1808, the very year that Dalton published his famous *New System of Chemical Philosophy*. But, as seems to be the case more than once in the history of science, the answer did not yet look like an answer, because chemists had not wrestled with the difficulties long enough yet to get the questions asked in exactly the right way.

What did Gay-Lussac discover? Monsieur Gay-Lussac worked with the combining volumes of gases. Notice, he was working with *volumes*, not (as Dalton) with *weights*. He discovered something, which reminded him of the observations of Proust. He noticed that the combining volumes of gases always seemed to turn out to be whole numbers.

He found that 2 volumes of carbonic oxide combined with 1 volume of oxygen to make 2 volumes of carbonic acid.

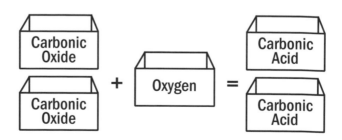

He noticed that 2 volumes of hydrogen and 1 volume of oxygen made 2 volumes of water (in the form of steam, the gaseous form of water).

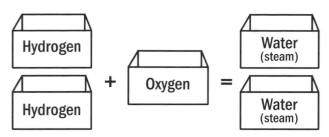

He observed that 3 volumes of hydrogen and 1 volume of nitrogen made 2 volumes of ammonia.

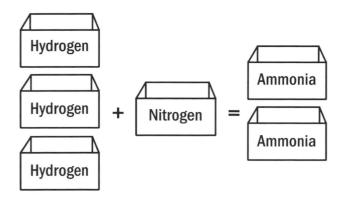

All whole numbers. Not a little bit over 1 volume of oxygen in carbonic acid, or just a tad under 2 volumes of hydrogen in water, or just a flea's eyelash over 1.12593032 volumes of nitrogen in ammonia, but 1, 2, and 1 exactly. All whole numbers. Very strange.

Furthermore, this soon led some to wonder whether equal volumes of different gases (under similar conditions of temperature and pressure) might contain the *same* number of particles. Why might such a notion occur?

Well, if you have 1 volume of hydrogen and 1 volume of chlorine (which, at the time, they called "oxygenated muriatic acid"), and they combine to make 2 volumes of hydrogen chloride (which they called "muriatic acid"), you might think that there would be exactly the same number of hydrogen atoms as chlorine atoms in the equal volumes.

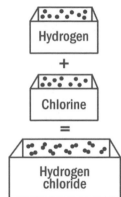

Two equal volumes combine to make twice their volume

But other things did not add up so nicely.

To return to one of our previous examples, if you think that equal volumes of different gases might contain the *same* number of particles, then this should happen:

1 volume of carbonic oxide + 1 volume of oxygen = 2 volumes of carbonic acid

But that was *not* what Gay-Lussac actually found. He found that,

2 volumes of carbonic oxide + 1 volume of oxygen = 2 volumes of carbonic acid

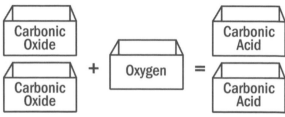

In fact, as lovely as Monsieur Gay-Lussac's experimental results were, no one could make sense of them.

Except one man, the Italian Amedeo Avogadro [ah vuh GAHD ro] (1776-1856).

AMADEO
AVOGADRO

Amedeo Avogadro published his answer in 1811, just three years after Dalton's book and Gay-Lussac's paper. He shouted the answer. But no one heard him. In fact, no one recognized the importance of his answer until 1860, almost fifty years later, when chemists were so fed up with all the problems and confusions plaguing chemistry that they called an international meeting. There, another Italian, Stanislao Cannizzaro (1826-1910), who did see the significance of Avogadro's answer, handed out a short pamphlet explaining it to the other chemists.

"Ahh," they said, "now we see!"

What did Avogadro see that cleared up the vision of his fellow chemists? That equal volumes of gases *do* indeed contain equal numbers of atoms, but some atoms travel in *pairs*. Once we realize that, declared Avagadro, we solve all the problems with Gay-Lussac's strange combining volumes, and all the problems with figuring out atomic weights too!

It all makes sense when we realize that, for example, oxygen likes to travel in pairs. So when we return to our example...

2 volumes of carbonic oxide + 1 volume of oxygen = 2 volumes of carbonic acid

And write it in modern symbols:

$$2CO + 1 \, O_2 = 2CO_2$$

Everything adds up perfectly.

In the 1 volume of oxygen, there were actually twice as many oxygen atoms as anyone had supposed. So if you had 1000 CO's in each volume, you would have 2000 CO's in two volumes. And if you had 1000 O_2's in one volume, you would actually have 2 x 1000 individual oxygen atoms, or 2000. Just enough to match up with the 2000 total CO's to make exactly 2 volumes of CO_2!

And hydrogen likes to travel in pairs as well, which is easy to see in regard to volumes of water (as steam) produced from their union.

$$2H_2 + O_2 = 2H_2O$$

And nitrogen likes to travel in pairs too, as we can see when hydrogen and nitrogen combine to form ammonia.

$$3H_2 + 1N_2 = 2NH_3$$

Finally, chlorine likes to travel in pairs as well, so what was really going on when chlorine combines with hydrogen was this:

$$1H_2 + 1Cl_2 = 2HCl$$

Once it was discovered that some elements always traveled in pairs *and* chemists had gotten more accurate calculations of the percentages of each element by weight in compounds, then things all fell into place.

To turn to the example of water, better calculations of the percentages by weight of oxygen and hydrogen in water were available in the mid 19th century. They found that water is 88.8% oxygen and 11.2% hydrogen. Recalling that chemists were calculating the weight of oxygen in relation to hydrogen, if we divide 88.8 by 11.2, we arrive at 7.92857 (rounded off). But when we realize that there are *two* hydrogen atoms and one oxygen atom in each water molecule, we know that *two* hydrogen atoms make up 11.2% of the weight. So a hydrogen atom will weigh $1/2$ this amount, which is the same as saying that one oxygen atom will weigh *twice* as much. And two times 7.92875 is 15.8575, which is very, very close to our contemporary relative weight of oxygen, 15.9994.

Fancy that it took so long to figure out just what water was made of—wouldn't Thales be proud!

As chemists accepted the insights of Avogadro, and used them to sort things out, they came into more and more agreement about the atomic weights of the elements, and the more agreement there was, the more accurately the atomic weights could be calculated.

We are now very, very close to our modern Periodic Table of Elements, and you may have even had a whisper of a hint about the next step, a step both so gigantic and so simple, that allowed the elements to be put in a definite order.

If you have all the elements, and each one has an

atomic weight, you might wonder if there is some kind of a *pattern* to the atomic weights? Some kind of beautiful, marvelous order just waiting, as a kind of intellectual treasure, to be discovered?

16. Things Fall Into Place: Triads and Octaves

Sometimes scientists try to make headway, and everything becomes more disordered and confusing. But sometimes scientists find far more order than they ever thought possible. Such times fill scientists with awe and wonder, as if they had gone digging for a few precious stones, and uncovered the vast treasure of a Pharaoh.

That is precisely what happened when chemists started to look for patterns in the atomic weights of the various elements. They were doing a very human thing. Human beings, especially scientists, but also philosophers and theologians, are always suspicious. They have a deep down feeling that things are not just put together randomly, a strange intuition that, underneath it all, there is a conspiracy going on, a great conspiracy of order. That is why chemists started to wonder, and wonder (as Aristotle said long ago) is the beginning of all science.

So, without knowing in advance whether it would lead to anything, chemists started to look for patterns among the elements, first small patterns, then larger patterns.

Johann Wolfgang Döbereiner [doh ber EYE ner] (1780-1849) noticed what he called "triads." These were groups of three elements, where the atomic weight of the "middle" element was (approximately) the mean of the lightest and heaviest of the three.

To make this clear, let us look at one of his triads: calcium (Ca), strontium (Sr), and barium (Ba). The weights Döbereiner used were calcium 27.5, strontium (about) 50, and barium 72.5. The mean is 47.25, which you get by adding the two extremes (27.5 + 72.5) and dividing by two. Well, that is about 50, the approximate atomic weight of strontium that he used, and Döbereiner thought it marvelous, especially when he found other triads. (We'll put them in vertical rows.)

1.Ca	1. Lithium (Li)	1. Sulfur (S)	1. Chlorine (Cl)
2. Sr	2. Sodium (Na)	2. Selenium (Se)	2. Bromine (Br)
3. Ba	3. Potassium (K)	3. Tellurium (Te)	3. Iodine (I)

Little did he know that he had stumbled upon a gold mine. If you look at the Periodic Table today, you can see that Döbereiner's triads run in vertical rows! (On our Table, the vertical rows are called *groups, and the horizontal rows are called *periods, so we'll use these terms from here on out.) Li, Na, and K line up very nicely right under hydrogen (H). In the very next vertical row, or group, the one with beryllium (Be) at the top, we find (after Magnesium, Mg), Ca, Sr, Ba lined up just like buttons on a coat! Then, scan over to the right hand side of the Table, to the group headed by oxygen (O), and right under it, lined up beautifully just like all the others, you will find S, Se, and Te. Go to the next group, to the right of S, and you find Cl, and under it, Br, and I. Marvelous indeed!

We should note, however, that Döbereiner's calculations were made on the basis of atomic weights *before* things were straightened out by Avagadro's insights. But, interestingly enough, Döbereiner found the *right* relations even with the *wrong* weights. To return to our first triad, the accepted atomic weight of calcium today is 40.08 (not 27.5), and barium's atomic weight is 137.34 (not 72.5). Yet, the mean of our two is 88.71, which is close to our accepted atomic weight of strontium, 87.62. The other triads listed above also work out fairly well. So he noticed the right *relation*, even if the atomic weights he used were in need of repair. (Before you jump to conclusions, such nice calculations don't work everywhere on our Table!)

So, Döbereiner's discovery was marvelous. Indeed, he did not know how marvelous it was, for the structure of the Table—the way the elements line up so precisely in groups and periods—had yet to be deciphered. He made a very good beginning, however.

Chemists tried to find all kinds of other relationships, always looking for patterns between the atomic weight and similarities in the properties of the elements. The single most important advance allowing chemists to find such patterns, as we may have guessed, was the use by Cannizzaro and others of Avagadro's insights which had cleared up all the confusions in regard to atomic weights. With this leap in accuracy at a little past the midpoint of the 19th century, came great intellectual leaps as well.

John Newlands (1837-1898) made a major *leap* forward by taking quite an obvious *step* forward: he simply took the known elements and arranged them, one after another, in order of increasing atomic weight, *and* numbered them accordingly, 1, 2, 3, 4, and so on, all the way up to 51. When he did, he noticed something rather odd: every 8th element had *similar* properties (or, at least, roughly similar properties).

He called it the Law of Octaves, because "the eighth element, starting from a given one, is a kind of repetition of the first, like the eighth note in an octave of music." **Do**, re, mi, fa, so, la, ti, **do**. Or using the letters, starting from middle C on a piano, **C**,

D, E, F, G, A, B, C. Every eighth element seemed to be a kind of repeat, since it shared similar properties with the first.

Let's take a look at his Table (published in 1866), and see not only how well he did, but how he accidentally stumbled upon the very heart of the order of the Table of Elements (without noticing it, however) merely by numbering the elements in accordance with increasing weight. (I've tilted Mr. Newlands' Table on its side, so that the elements run in the direction of our Table today. I have also included only part of it, the part which he got right! The rest of his table was not nearly as accurate.)

VII	I	II	III	IV	V	VI
1 H	2 Li	3 Be	4 B	5 C	6 N	7 O
8 F	9 Na	10 Mg	11 Al	12 Si	13 P	14 S
15 Cl	16 K	17 Ca				

Note that we have put Roman numerals above each group, *but* that we began with VII, then went on to I, II, and so on all the way up to VI. These are not Newlands' numbers, but correspond to the group numbers used today, which you find by looking at the top of the Table. If we take hydrogen (H) out and lay it to the side, and lift group VII up and put it down again where it belongs, to the right of group

VI, with F next to O, we see an amazing correspondence to our Table.

Again, what brought Newlands to the discovery of the Law of Octaves, was not just lining the elements up by increasing atomic weight, lightest to heaviest, but seeing the similar properties of every 8th element. So whatever element you chose, if you count from it like notes in a scale, either up or down, you end up in the same group, above or below the element from which you started.

For example, all the elements in group I (Li, Na, and K) are metals, and all are very, very reactive. They latch onto other elements and form compounds so quickly that they are never found alone in nature. Furthermore, a drop of water on any one of them will cause a violent reaction, even an explosion! Today, we call this group the Alkali Metals.

All the elements in group II (Be, Mg, Ca) likewise have similar properties. They are also metals and quite reactive. Today we call them the Alkaline-earth metals. Leaving hydrogen aside, the elements in group VII are called the halogens, which means "salt-formers," because they all readily combine with metals to make salts, the most famous being table salt, NaCl, sodium chloride.

Very good! Now for Mr. Newlands' accidental discovery. By *numbering* the elements according to their increasing atomic weight, Mr. Newlands accidentally stumbled upon the very heart of the order of the Periodic Table of Elements. If you look on today's Table, you see that the elements are numbered in horizontal rows, or periods, beginning with H as 1 and going all the way up to Mt (meitnerium) which is number 109. These are the *atomic numbers*. As we shall see in the next chapter, the atomic number, not the atomic weight, is the real key to the Table's wonderful order. At the time no one, not even Mr. Newlands himself, could see how merely numbering the elements in that way might be such a glorious key to unlocking the mystery of the Periodic Table of Elements. Chemists simply did not know enough yet.

To return to Mr. Newlands' Law of Octaves, when he did present it publicly, he struck a sour note, or rather, quite a few. As said above, we have included only part of his Table, about $^1/_3$ of it. The rest of it is not very accurate. A sign of this, even to the chemists of his day, was that the elements in the groups in the other $^2/_3$ of the chart he suggested as similar were not actually all that similar.

Poor John Newlands. A Mr. Carey Foster, whose only claim to fame is this one comment, sarcastically asked Newlands if he had thought of alphabetizing the elements instead.

But Newlands was on the right track, Mr. Carey Foster to the contrary. In fact, his elements would have lined up much better if he had only used the *first* draft of his chart instead of the second. In the first draft, he left blank spaces—gaps—where there were jumps in the atomic weights. He was too timid to leave such blank spaces in his second draft, the one he read before the members of the Chemical Society (which included Mr. Foster among the audience). After all, if he had blank spaces it would look as if there were holes in his chart where elements should be, blank spaces representing elements unknown but *waiting to be discovered!*

Such a thing would be bold! It would be outrageous! Predicting the discovery of unknown elements by their atomic weight! Such a thing was unheard of! Until along came Dimitrii Ivanovitch Mendeleev [men duh LAY eff] (1834-1907) who did that very thing.

Mr. Newlands might today be heralded as the discoverer of the Periodic Table of Elements if only he had *not* filled in those blank spaces, putting something where there was nothing. In this instance, the "nothing" was something more important than he could ever have guessed.

17. The Mystery Solved

Mr. Mendeleev was a Russian, born in cold Siberia, the youngest of 17 children (some say only 14). His father, a schoolteacher, became blind, and some time after, died. But his mother, who supported the family after the death of her husband by operating a glass factory, saw some great spark in young Dimitrii. She sacrificed everything and took him to learn science, first in Moscow, then in St. Petersburg, where he would later become a professor of chemistry.

Those of us who may never have heard of Mendeleev's famous ordering of the Periodic Table, may remember having seen a picture of him, for he is, with all due respect, a bit odd looking. In every picture or sketch we see him with his brilliant head sitting, so it seems, right on top of his shoulders, a wild beard framing the lower part of his face, and an even wilder head of hair framing the upper part. He is said to have cut his hair only once a year, when the weather turned hot, and it was so unruly that, as someone said of him, "every hair of his head seemed to act in independence of every other"!

DIMITRII
MENDELEEV

But his appearance aside, Mendeleev deserves every honor for finally figuring out the order of the elements on the Table, and even more interesting, using that order to predict the discovery of unknown elements where the "holes" were.

He discovered the order by playing cards. He wrote the properties of each element on separate cards, whether they were reactive or not reactive, or found in acids or bases, or were metals or non-metals, or combined with other elements in this way rather than that way. Then, he started to arrange them. And arranged them again. And rearranged the arranging until he noticed that, much as Newlands had realized (but quite imperfectly), the properties of the elements recurred *periodically*.

That is why it is called the Periodic Table, and why the horizontal rows are now called *periods*. When something recurs periodically, it repeats a pattern.

Like notes in a scale.

Or the numbers in our number system.

1	2	3	4	5	6	7	8	9	10
11	12	13	14	15	16	17	18	19	20

So the Periodic Table merely means that, for some mysterious reason, the elements are not just thrown together by nature in a jumble, but show very regular, astoundingly regular, patterns—if we are clever enough to uncover that underlying order.

Mendeleev was certainly clever. He published his first table, later called the Vertical Table, in 1869. If you wanted to compare it with our present-day Table, you would need to take it and rotate it a quarter of a turn, as we did with Newlands' table, so the columns would run up and down, rather than left to right.

But he published a second table in 1871 that runs horizontally just like our Table, and since he corrected some errors from the previous table, it is easier to compare it to ours.

It does differ from our modern Table, of course, but the basic structure is there. He started by putting hydrogen (H) outside everything else, in its own horizontal row, or period. That was important. As you can see from our modern Table, hydrogen stands alone as a kind of odd bird.

	I --- R^2O	II --- RO	III --- R^2O^3	IV RH^4 RO^2
1	H(1)			
2	Li(7)	Be(9.4)	B(11)	C(12)
3	Na(23)	Mg(24)	Al(27.3)	Si(28)
4	K(39)	Ca(40)	?(44)	Ti(48)
5	Cu(63)	Zn(65)	?(68)	?(72)
6	Rb(85)	Sr(87)	?Yt(88)	Zr(90)
7	Ag(108)	Cd(112)	In(113)	Sn(118)
8	Cs(133)	Ba(137)	?Di(138)	? Ce(140)
9	?	?	?	?
10	?	?	?Er(178)	?La(180)
11	Au(199)	Hg(200)	Tl(204)	Pb(207)
12	?	?	?	Th(231)

Mendeleev's Table of 1871

Then he just started putting the known elements in horizontal rows, or periods, by atomic weight, starting on the second row, which formed seven vertical columns, or groups, according to their common properties. In his table, there are twelve periods. In the diagram at the bottom of the opposite page we've shown the first six of his periods, boldfacing the elements he got right. (The atomic weights he used are in parentheses.)

V RH^3 R^2O^5	VI RH^2 RO^3	VII RH R^2O^7	VIII --- RO^4
N(14)	O(16)	F(19)	
P(31)	S(32)	Cl(35,5)	
V(51)	Cr(52)	Mn(55)	Fe(56) Co(59) Ni(59) Cu(63)
As(75)	Se(78)	Br(80)	
Nb(94)	Mo(96)	?(100)	Ru(104) Rh(104) Pd(106) Ag(108)
Sb(122)	Te(125)	J(127)	
?	?	?	? ? ? ?
?	?	?	
Ta(182)	W(184)	?	Os(195) Ir(197) Pt(198) Au(199)
Bi(208)	?	?	
?	U(240)	?	

I II III IV V VI VII

H (1)

I	II	III	IV	V	VI	VII
Li (7)	Be (9.4)	B (11)	C (12)	N (14)	O (16)	F (19)
Na (23)	Mg (24)	Al (27.3)	Si (28)	P (31)	S (32)	Cl(35.5)
K (39)	Ca (40)	? (44)	Ti (48)	V (51)	Cr (52)	Mn (55)
Cu (63)	Zn (65)	? (68)	? (72)	As (75)	Se (78)	Br (80)
Rb (85)	Sr (87)	Yt (88)	Zr (90)	Nb (94)	Mo (96)	? (100)

Let's pause here to make a few observations. First, Mendeleev's chart was not all that different from Mr. Newlands'. In fact, once Mr. Newlands got over his embarrassment at the hands of Mr. Foster, he wanted to be recognized as the real discoverer of the Periodic Table.

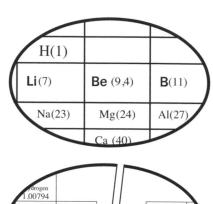

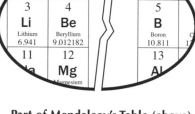

Part of Mendeleev's Table (above) compared with today's Table (below, with the gap in our table brought closer)

Second, Mendeleev's chart is very accurate until we come to the 4th period, beginning with potassium (K) and calcium (Ca). Everything checks out marvelously for the first, second, and third periods, the ones beginning H, Li, and Na. Even the atomic weights are very close to ours.

But when we get to the fourth period, the one beginning K, Ca, things do not line up very well, neither side to side, or up and down.

What happened?

Very simple. If we look on our modern Table we see what appears to be a long bridge connecting the elements on the left side with the elements on the right side. That long bridge is made up of the Transition Elements, and Mendeleev got mixed up because he did not yet know that this long bridge existed between groups II and III. But since he *did* know some of the elements which occur in the Transi-

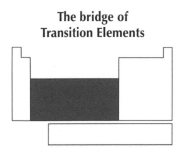

The bridge of Transition Elements

tion Elements bridge, he sometimes mistakenly put them at the wrong place.

There was another interesting and related problem. He had "leftover" elements, which he couldn't squeeze into the chart without knocking everything into confusion. He put these elements in another group, group VIII: Fe (56), Co (59), Ni (59). (Again, we are only looking at the top half of his Table.)

If he had known that there was such a "bridge" of Transition Elements between groups II and III, then he could have cleared up the problem very quickly. We can see this if we line up his period 4 with period 4 on our Table, then lift up Mendeleev's period 5 and patch it to his period 4, and finally pick up Fe (iron), Co (cobalt), and Ni (nickel) from group VIII, placing them between Mn (manganese) and Cu (copper). See next page.

K, Ca, ?, Ti, V, Cr, Mn, Fe, Co, Ni, etc.

(Mendeleev)

K, Ca, Sc, Ti, V, Cr, Mn, Fe, Co, Ni, etc.

(Ours)

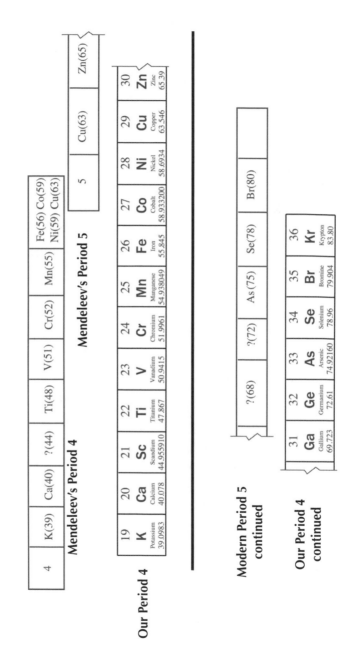

Our Period 4

| 4 | K(39) | Ca(40) | ?(44) | Ti(48) | V(51) | Cr(52) | Mn(55) | Fe(56) Co(59) Ni(59) Cu(63) | 5 | Cu(63) | Zn(65) |

Mendeleev's Period 4

Mendeleev's Period 5

19	20	21	22	23	24	25	26	27	28	29	30
K	**Ca**	**Sc**	**Ti**	**V**	**Cr**	**Mn**	**Fe**	**Co**	**Ni**	**Cu**	**Zn**
Potassium	Calcium	Scandium	Titanium	Vanadium	Chromium	Manganese	Iron	Cobalt	Nickel	Copper	Zinc
39.0983	40.078	44.955910	47.867	50.9415	51.9961	54.938049	55.845	58.933200	58.6934	63.546	65.39

Modern Period 5 continued

| ?(68) | ?(72) | As(75) | Se(78) | Br(80) |

Our Period 4 continued

31	32	33	34	35	36
Ga	**Ge**	**As**	**Se**	**Br**	**Kr**
Gallium	Germanium	Arsenic	Selenium	Bromine	Krypton
69.723	72.61	74.92160	78.96	79.904	83.80

Now things are lining up. Mendeleev probably would have gotten much closer, if he had only known more elements. A little more than half of our 109 elements were known at the time, and that made lining them up by atomic weight a bit tricky.

But Mendeleev did know enough to leave gaps in his table, and leaving gaps allowed him to guess where more elements *should* be.

We can see the question mark between Ca (calcium) and Ti (titanium), right where Sc (scandium) is today. Mendeleev knew there must be something in between Ca and Ti, but at the time, there was no known element that would "fit." That did not stop Mendeleev. He boldly predicted that one would be discovered, and even predicted, from its position in his table (in *his* group III), what some of its chemical properties would be. He even gave it a name (*eka boron*, "eka" meaning "first" in Sanskrit, and boron because its properties should resemble those of boron, B), and he gave it an atomic weight of 44.

Well, just as he predicted, *eka boron* was soon enough discovered. Lars Nilson, a Swede, discovered it in the mineral euxenite, and named it scandium (Sc, atomic weight 44.956) because scientists had only observed it in ores found in his native Scandinavia.

Looking at Mendeleev's Table, it makes sense that eka boron, lining up right under boron (B) and aluminum (Al) should have the same properties. But if we look at *our* Table, we find scandium (Sc) way over on the left next to calcium (Ca), and boron on the *other* side of the bridge, heading up group III.

While it is easy to see how Mendeleev could have guessed the correct atomic *weight* simply by the gaps left between the known elements, how could he have known that B and Sc would have similar *properties?* To make a complicated thing a bit simple, as far as many properties are concerned, the bridge of transition elements is a very smooth, and in many respects very slight transition, so that the properties of some of them are not all that different from those that occur either in group II or group III.

But we should not forget the simple truth that Mendeleev's chemical nose was very keen, leading him to see clearly what others could only see dimly (or not at all), even if the final version of the Table turned out differently.

It led him to suspect that two elements should exist between Zn (zinc) and As (arsenic), but again, no known elements fit the necessary atomic weights.

But that did not stop Mendeleev. "I shall call them *eka aluminum* and *eka silicon!*" For, as you might already have guessed, he thought the unknown elements would have the general properties of the already-known elements of aluminum and silicon. "Furthermore, their atomic weights shall be 68 and 72."

And they were found. In 1875, Paul Lecoq de Boisbaudran [leh COCK de bwah ba DRAWN] discovered *eka aluminum*, but since he was a great patriot of France he called it gallium (Ga, atomic weight 69.72), for France's Gallic heritage. (Some suggest that Monsieur Lecoq was even more sly, for Lecoq was a bit of a Chanticleer, *gallus* being the Latin name of the crowing cock.)

In 1886, Clemens Winkler discovered *eka silicon*, but he called it germanium (Ge, atomic weight 72.59), for he thought his people, the Germans, were every bit as clever as the French!

But not only did Mendeleev use his table to predict the discovery of previously unknown elements, he used it to correct the accepted atomic weights of elements. For example, the accepted atomic weight of a recently discovered element indium (In). The accepted atomic weight would put it between Ar (arsenic) and Se (selenium), but there was no room between the two, and furthermore, the properties of indium did not fit that place in the table. Looking at its properties, Mendeleev declared that it must be between Cd (cadmium) and Sn (tin), right where we find it today! He did the same for U (uranium) and Au (gold). The recalculated weights fit!

Now that does not mean that Mendeleev always predicted accurately, but he did much of the time, and that gave others the confidence to adopt his system (and correct his errors). Once his system was accepted, elements began to be discovered left and right, whether he predicted them or not.

In relation to the magnitude of his correct insights, the size of his errors is rather small by comparison. That is why Mendeleev is credited with establishing the modern Periodic Table of the Elements. When he died in 1907, his students carried huge Periodic Table placards in the funeral procession. And, if you look at element 101 near the end of the second row in the double strip of elements running along the bottom of the Periodic Table, you will find Md, Mendelevium, named after Mendeleev himself. Mendelevium is not, however, a natural element, but an artificial one. It was created in 1955 by a team of scientists in California.

And Mr. Mendeleev, you deserve to have an element named after you for doing so much to unravel the mystery of the Periodic Table of Elements. But of course, we know that you could not have done it without a whole army of alchemists and chemists stretching all the way back to that first lucky human being to have discovered the shining nugget of gold on the river bank.

RUTHERFORD

18. The Mystery Continues

I.

With Mr. Mendeleev we have gotten the *logic* of the Periodic Table. Or, at least, we might say we have the *general* logic. Why?

Because the *general* order of the rows Mendeleev discovered through lining up the elements by atomic weight is correct, but lining them up by atomic weight, oddly enough, is not. As with so many before him in the history of science, he got the right answer, but not exactly for the right reason!

Mendeleev could not have gotten the right reason, however. The real cause of the beautiful order of the Periodic Table required the destruction of Dalton's indestructible atoms. The reason that the elements line up so nicely was only found at the beginning of the 20th century, when scientists broke through the unbreakable atom and began to investigate the *sub*-atomic level, the level of protons, electrons, and neutrons. Neither Dalton nor Mendeleev could ever have imagined such things!

We remember that Humphry Davy made clear that the elements have some kind of electrical charge, both positive and negative. But what was the cause? Were there different *parts* to the atom? That would be very strange, since atoms weren't supposed to have any parts!

Scientists did have some clues. About the mid-19th century they discovered that electricity moving through a tube of gas (at low pressure) produced a kind of beam. The "beam" came from the electrode at one end called a "cathode." Julius Plücker (1801-1868), a professor of physics and mathematics at Bonn, Germany, found something very interesting about this beam. It could be moved by a magnet! In 1897, Joseph John Thomson (1856-1940), an Englishman, proved conclusively that the beam made by the cathode ray tube (as it was called) could be moved by a magnet because it consisted of *negatively* charged particles.

Aha! So whatever these particles were, they must

be the source of the negative charge that chemists had known about for over a half a century. These particles came to be called "electrons."

ERNEST
RUTHERFORD

But what about the positive charge? Another Englishman, Ernest Rutherford (1871-1937), found the source of the positive charge, and also something very odd about the atom itself. In 1911, he directed a beam of alpha particles (which he knew to be positively charged) at a thin metal foil. Oddly enough, most passed right through as if nothing were there. But a very few bounced back!

Bounced back? Rutherford was astounded! "It was quite the most incredible thing that ever happened to me in my life," he said, "as if you had fired a 15-inch shell at a piece of tissue paper and it came back and hit you."

What happened? Have you ever tried to put the north ends of two magnets together? If you put them on the table, and push one at the other, they bounce away from each other. That is exactly what happened to Rutherford. Very few of the alpha particles bounced back, so Rutherford knew that the positive alpha particles that did bounce back were bouncing off something very, very small. But that very, very small thing was powerfully, positively charged.

These very small positively charged particles of the atom were called "protons." Rutherford was astounded because the places where the positive alpha particles did bounce back were extraordinarily small compared to the whole metal sheet. This indicated that, in the atoms of metal, the protons must be concentrated in very, very small places, and so must be very, very small parts of each atom. He believed that the protons were at the center, or the nucleus, of each atom of the metal, and the electrons surrounded that nucleus.

Just how small is the positively charged nucleus of the atom relative to the size of the whole atom? We cannot possibly represent it in this book! The radius of the whole atom is about 10,000 times greater than the radius of the nucleus. If the nucleus were the size of a baseball, the outermost "edge" of the atom would be a third of a mile away! If the nucleus were as small as the dot on this "i" then the "edge" of the atom would be as big as a garage!

Small wonder that Rutherford thought that his results were "quite the most incredible thing that ever happened to me in my life." It is reported that he was so astounded, that he immediately danced the *haka* of the New Zealand Maori, a rather violent stomping and yelling dance which Maori men perform before they go into battle. If you have ever seen the *haka* danced, and you have also seen a picture of the very serious and somber Sir Ernest Rutherford, First Baron of Nelson and Cambridge, you might find Mr. Rutherford's joyous *haka* nearly as astounding as the nature of the atom!

One wonders what kind of dance Mr. Rutherford would have performed if he had come upon what another Englishman, Henry Moseley (1887-1915), discovered just two years later. By x-raying various metals, Moseley found out that the wavelengths of the different elements revealed a quite surprising and magnificent order, an order which corresponded *directly* to the order of the Periodic Table. After carefully analyzing the X-ray spectra, he was able to show that *the positive charge of each element's nucleus increases by one as you move from one element to the next.*

Not by a little over one, or a tad under one. The positive charge increased by *exactly* one.

The key to the order of the Table was beautifully, wonderfully, marvelously exact. Hydrogen had one proton, and each element after that had one more proton in its nucleus than the one before it.

Mendeleev thought that the key was atomic weight. Moseley showed that the real cause of the underlying order was not atomic weight, but the number of protons which each element has. But we must stress one very important fact: Moseley could never have gotten the answer without Mendeleev.

Before we look at the atom and the Periodic Table in more detail, we must note that there was another important part of the atom yet to be discovered, the neutron, but its discovery would not occur for another two decades after Moseley. Scientists discovered it because the weight, or mass, of the atom, was not adding up properly.

Electrons had barely any mass at all, and protons had only about half the mass needed. Scientists had already found the sources of the positive and negative electrical charges of the atom. Could there be some part of the atom that had the needed mass, but no electrical charge?

Indeed. The neutron, which has no charge, but is electrically neutral (hence the name). As it turns out, it is slightly heavier than a proton and 1,838 times as heavy as the electron. A perfect fit!

No doubt this all seems rather hard to grasp, but if we look at a particular example of an element—let's use carbon—it will all become clear, and we shall begin to see how the subatomic world is the real key to the order of the Periodic Table.

We will use $\oplus$ for the proton, since it has a positive electrical charge; $\ominus$ for the electron, since it has a negative electrical charge, and **O** for the neutron, since it has no electrical charge at all.

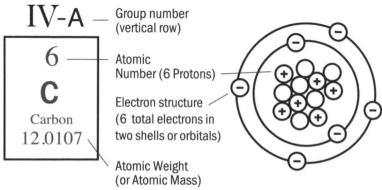

IV-A — Group number (vertical row)

6 — Atomic Number (6 Protons)

C — Electron structure (6 total electrons in two shells or orbitals)

Carbon

12.0107 — Atomic Weight (or Atomic Mass)

The atomic number refers to the number of *protons* in the nucleus of the atom. For carbon (C) it is 6, for oxygen (O) it is 8, for Lead (Pb) it is 82.

So, if you start at hydrogen (H), with atomic number 1, then go to helium (He), with atomic number 2, then on to lithium (Li) with atomic number 3, and so on, you are just counting from 1 to 109 in horizontal rows of elements by atomic number, the number of protons which each element has.

And again, *that* is the real reason why the elements line up horizontally, *not* because of atomic weight.

If we go to tellurium (Te) with atomic

	Selenium 78.96	Bromine 79.904	Kryp... 83.80
1	**52**	**53**	**54**
b	**Te**	**I**	**Xe**
ony	Tellurium 127.60	Iodine 126.90447	Xenon 131.29
0	84	85	8

Iodine's atomic weight is less than Tellurium's

number 52 and atomic *weight* of 127.6, we can see the problem of lining up elements by atomic weight. The next element in line is iodine (I) with atomic *number* 53 but atomic *weight* of 126.904. The number of protons has gone up by one, but for very complex reasons (beyond the scope of this book to explain) the atomic weight has *dropped!*

We should also note that, since the atomic numbers are always whole numbers (1, 2, 3, 4, and so on), they are quite exact, and therefore much easier to deal with than atomic weights (1.0079, 4.0026, 6.939, 9.0122 and so on).

But why do the elements line up *vertically*?

Very simple (although, like almost everything else, it was not so easy to discover). While the number of protons tells us how elements line up one after another horizontally, if that were all that we had, our Table of Elements would be just one, long horizontal row.

1	2	3	4	5	6	7	8
H	**He**	**Li**	**Be**	**B**	**C**	**N**	**O**
Hydrogen	Helium	Lithium	Beryllium	Boron	Carbon	Nitrogen	Oxygen
1.00794	4.003	6.941	9.012182	10.811	12.0107	14.00674	15.9994

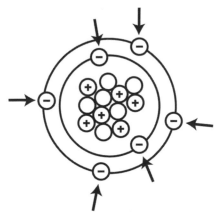

The number and structure of electrons around the nucleus of Carbon

And so on, until all the way to Meitnerium, (Mt) with atomic number 109, having (of course) 109 protons.

But that is not what we find, and the reason for this is the number and structure of the *electrons* around the nucleus of protons and neutrons.

We recall that Mendeleev (and Newlands before him) saw that, when the elements were put in order of increasing atomic *weight*, periodic similarities be-

9	10	11	12	13	14	15	16
F	**Ne**	**Na**	**Mg**	**Al**	**Si**	**P**	**S**
Fluorine	Neon	Sodium	Magnesium	Aluminum	Silicon	Phosphorus	Sulfur
18.9984032	20.1797	22.989770	24.3050	26.981538	28.0855	30.973761	32.066

tween properties of the elements appeared, and these periodic similarities allowed the elements to be aligned in *vertical* rows, or groups: IA, IIA, IIIA, IVA, VA, VIA, and VIIA. (Note that we're now adding "A" to the groups, to distinguish them from the vertical rows in the Transitional Elements.)

What caused the similar properties? The electrons, which of course Mendeleev could not have known anything about, for they had not been discovered yet.

The number of electrons and their positions in shells appear on the right hand side of each element on the Table. Let us look at vertical column IA to see the pattern.

First we notice that, for each element, the number of electrons is *equal* to the number of protons:

Electron structure for group I<small>A</small>

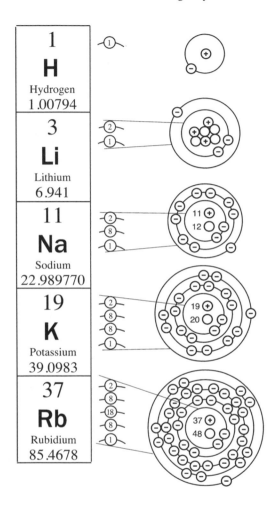

1 **H** Hydrogen 1.00794	
3 **Li** Lithium 6.941	
11 **Na** Sodium 22.989770	
19 **K** Potassium 39.0983	
37 **Rb** Rubidium 85.4678	

Then we notice that the *last* number to be added is always 1. That is the reason all the elements in Group I<small>A</small> have the same properties—they all have 1 electron in what is called the outermost electron "shell" around the nucleus. (Think of the atom as an

Continuation: Electron structure for group IA

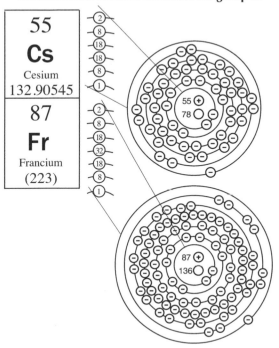

Group IA Element	Protons (atomic number)	Electrons
H (hydrogen)	1	1
Li (lithium)	3	3 (2+1)
Na (sodium)	11	11 (2+8+1)
K	19	19 (2+8+8+1)
Rb (rubidium)	37	37 (2+8+18+8+1)
Cs (cesium)	55	55 (2+8+18+18+8+1)
Fr (francium)	87	87 (2+8+18+32+18+8+1)

onion where the shells are layers around the core, the last or outermost layer being the outer shell—a somewhat helpful, but not very exact picture, as will soon become clear.) All the elements in Group IA are very reactive (they lose their one electron very easily), they all have a low density, and they are all classed as soft metals. Again, the elements in this group are called the alkali metals.

We find this pattern in all the Groups from IA to VIIA (excluding, for now, the Transition Element bridge). If, for example, we return to the picture of our carbon atom above, we can see that there are 2 electrons in the "shell" closest to the nucleus, and 4 electrons in the outermost shell. *That* is precisely why carbon is in the vertical column marked IVA—it has four electrons in its outermost shell.

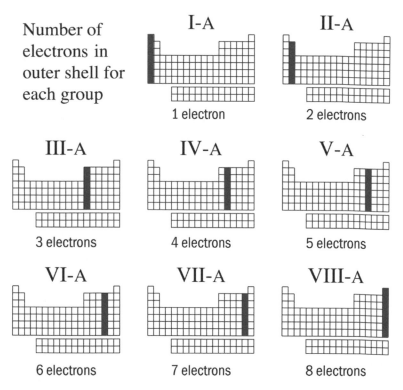

Number of electrons in outer shell for each group

I-A
1 electron

II-A
2 electrons

III-A
3 electrons

IV-A
4 electrons

V-A
5 electrons

VI-A
6 electrons

VII-A
7 electrons

VIII-A
8 electrons

It is a very simple and beautiful pattern.

All the elements in Group IA have 1 electron in the outer shell.

All the elements in Group IIA have 2 electrons in the outer shell.

Leaping over to IIIA we find that all its elements from B (boron) down to thalium (Tl) have 3 electrons in the outer shell.

And so on as we move toward the right-hand side, when we get to Group VIIA, where all the elements from fluorine (Fl) down to astatine (At) have 7 electrons in the outer shell.

One column over from that, the very last vertical column, Group VIIIA, is that of the Noble Gases, something else Mendeleev never dreamed of. They are called the Noble Gases because they are rather stand-offish; that is, they don't like to mingle with the other elements. In a word, they are non-reactive, and so don't like to combine with other elements, as if they were somehow aristocratically aloof.

Although our Mr. Cavendish stumbled upon the Noble Gas argon (Ar) in 1783, he did not recognize it. It was not until 1894 that argon was actually recognized as a distinct element, and the discovery of the entire group VIIIA was completed by 1900 when radon (Rn) was discovered.

What makes the Noble Gases so stand-offish, so aloof, so unreactive? Each of them has 8 electrons in its outer shell, and that makes a shell full. Since their outer shells are full, the Noble Gases do not care either to give or receive any electrons. Thus, if we want to add an electron, we must start in a new shell, and that will always take us back to Group IA again, the next period down.

For example, Neon (Ne), with atomic number 10, has the *second* shell filled with 8 electrons, so that if we want to add an electron, we need to open another shell on the next horizontal row, period 3, beginning with sodium (Na). Sodium starts the *third* shell with 1 electron.

Let's keep going. Add another proton, neutron, and electron, and you have magnesium (Mg).

Add another proton, neutron, and electron to Mg and you get aluminum (Al).

Keep adding a proton, neutron, and electron until you get all the way over to argon (Ar) and the 3rd electron shell will be full!

Time to start another horizontal row with potassium (K).

Things work wonderfully well until we get to the Transition Element bridge, where they do follow a kind of order, but not nearly as clear. Things only become "normal" again, when we have crossed the bridge and are at gallium (Ga) in Group IIIA. Here we find (as we did with boron and aluminum), that gallium's outer shell has three electrons. The same irregularity with the Transition Elements is found in the rest of the Table. And worse yet, that band of elements at the bottom, the Inner Transition Elements, must be squeezed into the Transition Elements bridge, right after lanthanum (La) with atomic number 57, and actinium (Ac) with atomic number 89. We'll make some sense of these oddities in a moment. But first, we must return to the clearer parts of the Table. So for now, let's turn our attention to the neutron and atomic weights.

We have not said much about the neutrons yet. While the protons line elements up horizontally, and the electrons line things up vertically, what is there left for the poor neutrons to do?

As already mentioned above, they help to make up the weight (or mass) of the atom. The electrons barely contribute anything to the weight of an atom. The protons and neutrons together make up almost all of an atom's atomic weight.

The relative weight of a proton is 1.00727 (relative to carbon, not hydrogen, as we'll soon see).

The relative weight of an electron is .000549.

The relative weight of a neutron is 1.00867.

Now everything would be much easier if only the neutrons would behave themselves. But whereas you find an equal number of protons and electrons in an atom of the same element, the number of neutrons varies.

For example, a carbon (C) atom will have 6 protons, but may have only 5 neutrons. Or 6. Or 7. Or 8.

Each of these atoms of carbon will have a different atomic weight—a bit more for every neutron that is added.

The number of neutrons in an atom of the same element varies

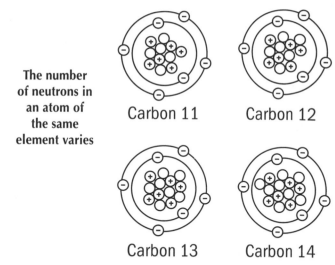

Carbon 11   Carbon 12

Carbon 13   Carbon 14

When the same element can have different numbers of neutrons, these forms of the element are called an element's *isotopes* (from the Greek, "same-place," since they are on the same place on the Periodic Table, rather than being a new or different element). Above we have listed isotopes of carbon: carbon 11, carbon 12, carbon 13, and carbon 14.

Each isotope will have a slightly different atomic weight, and the weight that you find on the Table under each element is calculated from its isotopes (in a rather complicated manner).

And, by the way, the atomic weights are still *relative*, as they were for Dalton, but not relative to the weight of hydrogen. They are all relative to the weight of an isotope of carbon, carbon 12. The atomic weight of carbon 12 is taken to be *exactly* 12, and everything else, including hydrogen, is given its weight relative to carbon 12.

While there are 109 elements, there are over 1000 isotopes!

Not only do protons, electrons, and neutrons help us to understand the logic of the Table. They also make it very clear why discovering that elements and compounds had positive and negative electrical charges was so important. The shocking Mr. Davy's suspicion that, because electrolysis caused elements and compounds to be attracted either to the negative or positive poles, the elements themselves must somehow be electrically positive and negative, turned out to be exactly right. Furthermore, Davy's battering compounds apart by electrical currents makes sense if it is electrical attraction that is binding those elements together.

II.

Now what about the murkier parts of the Table, the strange Transition Element bridge, and the even stranger Inner Transition elements squeezed into the Transition Elements? Let's take the bridge first.

If we scan across the Transition Element bridge, looking at the number of electrons in the outermost shell of each element, we notice something very interesting.

21	22	23	24	25	26	27	28	29	30
Sc	**Ti**	**V**	**Cr**	**Mn**	**Fe**	**Co**	**Ni**	**Cu**	**Zn**
Scandium	Titanium	Vanadium	Chromium	Manganese	Iron	Cobalt	Nickel	Copper	Zinc
44.955910	47.867	50.9415	51.9961	54.938049	55.845	58.933200	58.6934	63.546	65.39
2	2	2	2	2	2	2	2	2	2
8	8	8	8	8	8	8	8	8	8
9	10	11	13	13	14	15	16	18	18
2	2	2	1	2	2	2	2	1	2

While the number of electrons in the outermost shell is always 1 or 2, the *second to last* shell is the one (almost always) rising, or filling up.

In period 4, for example, we see the second to last shell filling up until it finally gets to 18 at zinc (Zn), at the very end of the Transition Element bridge. With the next element, gallium (Ga), we are in Group IIIA, where we expect to find 3 electrons in the *outer* shell—and so we do! Now, we simply continue adding one electron to the *outer* shell as we

Looking at the Inner Transition Elements

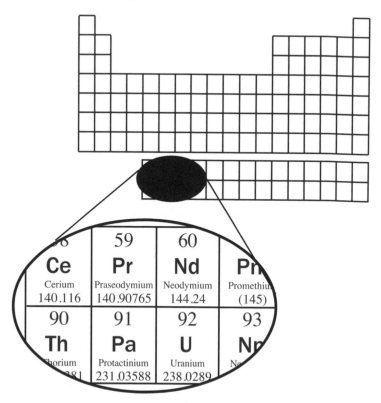

march across from germanium (Ge) to krypton (Kr), where we have completed the outer shell with 8 electrons and are ready to go down a row, and begin the next period, period 5, with rubidium (Rb).

Not too confusing. The fundamental difference can be boiled down to this: the main elements (Groups IA through VIIIA) fill up the *outermost* electron shell, while the Transition Elements fill up one of the *inner* electron shells (called subshells).

What about the Inner Transition Elements, the so-called Lanthanide and Actinide series floating there at the bottom of the Table?

Fear not. Recall that they are squeezed into the Transition Element bridge. That tells us that somehow, they are going to fill up *inner* rather than outer electron shells as we march across from element to element.

Note again, how the Inner Transition elements are squeezed in: elements 57 through 71, the elements of the Lanthanide series, have to fit into the little space between barium (Ba) and hafnium (Hf). Elements 89 through 103, the elements of the Actinide series, must be wedged into the little gap between radium (Ra) and rutherfordium (Rf).

If we look at the electron shell structure as we scan across these elements*, we see right away that an inner shell is being filled up with electrons as we move from left to right, not the second to last shell, however, but *third* to last shell.

* See next two pages.

57	58	59	60	61	62	63	64
La	**Ce**	**Pr**	**Nd**	**Pm**	**Sm**	**Eu**	**Gd**
Lanthanum	Cerium	Praseodymium	Neodymium	Promethium	Samarium	Europium	Gadolinium
138.9055	140.116	140.90765	144.24	(145)	150.36	151.964	157.25
2	2	2	2	2	2	2	2
8	8	8	8	8	8	8	8
18	18	18	18	18	18	18	18
18	20	21	22	23	24	25	25
9	8	8	8	8	8	8	9
2	2	2	2	2	2	2	2

By the time we get to lutetium (Lu), we have finally filled up that shell completely with 32 electrons, and are ready to return to the Transition Element bridge with hafnium (Hf), and pick up the pattern of filling the *second* to last shell again.

So, there we have it.

We know the reason for the structure of the Periodic Table of Elements.

Is that the end of the story?

No. Not in the least, because that is not the end of the mystery!

The deeper scientists dig, the more mysterious things turn out to be. The atomic world is strange enough; the sub-atomic world is stranger still.

Have we even reached the end of the number of elements?

Not at all. We do not know how many elements there might be because we have taken to making them ourselves! The last, heaviest, naturally occurring element is number 92, uranium (U). Element

65	66	67	68	69	70	71
Tb	**Dy**	**Ho**	**Er**	**Tm**	**Yb**	**Lu**
Terbium	Dysprosium	Holmium	Erbium	Thulium	Ytterbium	Lutetium
158.92534	162.50	164.93032	167.26	168.93421	173.04	174.967
2	2	2	2	2	2	2
8	8	8	8	8	8	8
18	18	18	18	18	18	18
27	28	29	30	31	32	32
8	8	8	8	8	8	9
2	2	2	2	2	2	2

93, neptunium (Np), was produced artificially in 1940 (although scientists have since identified very small amounts of Np occurring naturally, so we might put Np rather than U as the last natural element). Beyond Np, all the rest of the elements are artificially produced as well. And so, scientists have stretched the Periodic Table beyond element 109, meitnerium (Mt), by making even heavier elements.

Element 110 is called ununnilium (Uun), and it was claimed to have been made in 1994 (at the same laboratory that made elements 107, 108, and 109!). The name ununnilium simply means "110-ium," a name used until they think of something more fitting. It was created by fusing the nuclei of lead (Pb) and nickel (Ni) atoms, which makes perfect sense mathematically.

Nickel has 28 protons and lead has 82 protons. If you add them (i.e., fuse them) you get 110 protons, and a new element, "110-ium."

Easy mathematically, but it took 10 years to do it,

and only four or five atoms of Uun were made. These atoms were so unstable, that they fell apart (or decayed) after a half of a thousandth of a second!

Element 111? Unununium (Uuu), created just a month after Uun. Only three atoms of Uuu were made, and it was done by "adding" nickel (28) and bismuth (83), to get 111 protons in the Uuu nucleus. Alas, the three atoms of Uuu were only around for a fraction of a fraction of a second.

Element 112? Ununbiium (Uub), made in 1996— but only one atom of it! How did they get it? By "adding" zinc (30) with lead (82) to get a nucleus with 112 protons.

Element 113? I've not heard anything yet. Have you?

In 1999, Russian scientists reported making element 114, ununquadium (Uuq), one atom of it.

Element 115? No news here.

Element 116, ununhexium (Uuh) was reportedly made in 1999 as a by-product of the creation of element 118, ununoctium (Uuo) by scientists in California, but whether these elements were indeed created is still a matter of controversy. Time will tell.

Simply put, we do not yet know the limit of making atoms of new elements artificially, and because these high-number artificial elements decay so rapidly, we do not even know much at all about the ones that have been made. How far we can go, and what these elements are like, are mysteries.

But these are not the only mysteries with which

we are faced.

The structure of the atom as we have pictured it is, to say the very least, enormously simplified. Real electrons, for example, are not nice little round balls flitting around perfectly round orbits. They are an odd combination of a wave and a particle, which leaps about in ways that we have great difficulties understanding.

Also, remember how astounded Mr. Rutherford was to find that the atoms, out of which every material thing in the universe is made, seem to be made mostly of empty space!

That is very mysterious, indeed. Perhaps someday, we shall find that it is filled with something even more mysterious. Perhaps not. We do not now know.

And that is not all.

We cannot picture the number of sub-atomic particles, because beyond electrons, protons, and neutrons, there are positrons, neutrinos, and photons.

And mesons, muons, and pions.

And hundreds and hundreds of other very small and very, very strange particles, all of which make up the atoms of the elements.

Scientists have been trying to classify them, just as they classified the elements, and that is leading to *another* Table.

But the order of *that* Table is a mystery that scientists are thick in the middle of trying to solve.

Glossary

Acid
: Acids taste sour or tart, and change litmus to red. In contemporary chemical understanding, they are defined as proton donors because they donate hydrogen ions.

Alloy
: A substance composed of two or more metals (for example, bronze, from copper and tin), or one or more metals and certain non-metals, especially carbon (for example, steel, from iron and carbon).

Base
: Bases taste bitter, are slippery to the touch, and change litmus to blue. In contemporary chemical understanding, they are defined as proton acceptors because they accept hydrogen ions.

Calcination
: When metals are burned in air, a whitish powder forms upon them, which the alchemists called "calx," from the Latin word for lime or chalk. Later, it was discovered that

the white chalky substance is caused by the addition of oxygen to the metal during burning.

Compound   A substance of more than one element.

Conservation
of Mass   In its first formulation by Lavoisier, the law of conservation of mass (or of matter) states that in every reaction there is an equal quantity of matter before and after the operation, or more simply, in a chemical reaction, the total amount of matter of the reaction compounds remains constant.

Distillation   Distillation separates liquid compounds into elements or simpler compounds by vaporizing (using fire) or evaporation (using the sun).

Element   For practical purposes, most chemistry books today define an element as a substance which cannot be broken down by chemical change into simpler, purer substances. The difficulty, however, consists in defining both "chemical change" and "substance." Is using a cyclotron, an enormous round device that creates a strong magnetic field and an electric field to accelerate particles to high velocities for bombardment, a "chemical change"? Is Mendelevium (element 101), which was built artificially, one atom at a time, and which so little of it has been made that little is known of it, a "substance"? For these reasons, chemists also define an "element" more exactly as all atoms with the same number of protons.

Groups   The vertical rows on the Periodic Table.

Law of Definite
Proportions   Formulated by Proust, the law states that in a compound, the constituent elements are always present in a definite proportion by weight.

Law of Multiple
Proportions   Dalton's Law of Multiple Proportions states that "In the formation of two or more compounds from the same elements, the weights of one element that combine with a fixed weight of a second element are in a ratio of small whole numbers (integers) such as 2 to 1, 3 to 1, 3 to 2, or 4 to 3."

Mass	Mass is not the same as weight. The mass of an object takes into account not only the amount of matter that a body contains but also the resistance that body has to change in its motion (called "inertia"). A body may weigh twenty pounds on Earth, but weigh nothing as it floats out in space. But both on Earth and in space, the body will have mass.
Ores	An ore is a naturally occurring rock, or mineral combination, with a high concentration of metals.
Periods	The horizontal rows on the Periodic Table.
Reduction	Reduction occurs when elements are removed from a compound, as when, for example, the oxygen is removed from iron oxide, leaving only iron.
Smelting	Smelting is a process by which ore is heated to extract the pure metal. In the process of smelting, the ore is heated with a reducing agent and a flux to remove the unwanted elements, leaving the desired pure metal.

The Elements in Order
of Their Discovery

The following is a list of the elements according to the historical order in which they were discovered. As far as possible, these discovery dates reflect the date on which each element was *isolated*, and not always the date on which it was properly *identified*. So, for example, Cavendish is normally credited with isolating hydrogen in 1766, but as we know from Chapter 10, it was Lavoisier who properly identified it about 10 years later. A good up-to-date resource on the elements, including the discovery of new elements, can be found at www.webelements.com.

Of course, we cannot affix a date to the discovery of the very common elements. Prior to 1600 AD the elements gold, silver, mercury, copper, lead, tin, iron, sulfur, carbon, arsenic, antimony, bismuth, and zinc were all known.

Known prior to 1600

Gold	Au	79
Silver	Ag	47
Copper	Cu	29
Carbon	C	6
Iron	Fe	26
Lead	Pb	82

Tin	Sn	50
Sulfur	S	16
Mercury	Hg	80
Arsenic	As	33
Antinomy	Sb	51
Bismuth	Bi	83
Zinc	Zn	30

Discovered or isolated after 1600 (divided into centuries)

1669	Phosphorus	P	15
1737	Cobalt	Co	27
1748	Platinum	Pt	78
1751	Nickel	Ni	28
1766	Hydrogen	H	1
1772	Nitrogen	N	7
1774	Chlorine	Cl	17
1774	Manganese	Mn	25
1774	Oxygen	O	8
1781	Molybdenum	Mo	42
1783	Tellurium	Te	52
1783	Tungsten	W	74
1791	Titanium	Ti	22
1794	Yttrium	Y	39
1798	Chromium	Cr	24
1801	Niobium	Nb	41
1802	Tantalum	Ta	73
1803	Palladium	Pd	46

1803	Rhodium	Rh	45
1803	Cerium	Ce	58
1804	Osmium	Os	76
1804	Iridium	Ir	77
1807	Potassium	K	19
1807	Sodium	Na	11
1808	Barium	Ba	56
1808	Strontium	Sr	38
1808	Calcium	Ca	20
1808	Magnesium	Mg	12
1808	Boron	B	5
1811	Iodine	I	53
1817	Lithium	Li	3
1817	Cadmium	Cd	48
1818	Selenium	Se	34
1824	Silicon	Si	14
1824	Zirconium	Zr	40
1825	Aluminum	Al	13
1825	Bromine	Br	35
1828	Beryllium	Be	4
1829	Thorium	Th	90
1841	Lanthanum	La	57
1841	Uranium	U	92
1843	Terbium	Tb	65
1843	Erbium	Er	68
1844	Ruthenium	Ru	44
1860	Cesium	Cs	55
1861	Rubidium	Rb	37
1861	Thallium	Tl	81
1863	Indium	In	49

1867	Vanadium	V	23
1875	Gallium	Ga	31
1878	Holmium	Ho	67
1878	Ytterbium	Yb	70
1879	Thulium	Tm	69
1879	Scandium	Sc	21
1879	Samarium	Sm	62
1880	Gadolinium	Gd	64
1885	Praseodymium	Pr	59
1885	Neodymium	Nd	60
1886	Germanium	Ge	32
1886	Fluorine	F	9
1886	Dysprosium	Dy	66
1894	Argon	Ar	18
1895	Helium	He	2
1898	Krypton	Kr	36
1898	Neon	Ne	10
1898	Xenon	Xe	54
1898	Polonium	Po	84
1898	Radium	Ra	88
1899	Actinium	Ac	89
1900	Radon	Rn	86
1901	Europium	Eu	63
1907	Lutetium	Lu	71
1917	Protactinium	Pa	91
1923	Hafnium	Hf	72
1925	Rhenium	Re	75
1939	Francium	Fr	87
1939	Technetium	Tc	43

1940	Neptunium	Np	93
1940	Astatine	At	85
1940	Plutonium	Pu	94
1944	Americium	Am	95
1944	Curium	Cm	96
1945	Promethium	Pm	61
1949	Berkelium	Bk	97
1949	Californium	Cf	98
1952	Einsteinium	Es	99
1952	Fermium	Fm	100
1955	Mendelevium	Md	101
1958	Nobelium	No	102
1961	Lawrencium	Lr	103
1969	Rutherfordium	Rf	104
1970	Dubnium	Db	105
1974	Seaborgium	Sg	106
1981	Bohrium	Bh	107
1982	Meitnerium	Mt	109
1984	Hassium	Hs	108
1994	Ununnilium	Uun	110
1994	Unununium	Uuu	111
1996	Ununbiium	Uub	112
1999	Ununhexium	Uuh	116
1999	Ununoctium	Uuo	118

About the Author

Benjamin Wiker received his doctorate in Theological Ethics from Vanderbilt University, and has taught at Marquette University, St. Mary's University (MN), and Thomas Aquinas College. He now writes full time, and teaches part time at Franciscan University in Steubenville, OH. He has published another book, *Moral Darwinism: How We Became Hedonists*, and writes for a number of national journals. Dr. Wiker is also a Senior Fellow at the Discovery Institute, the think-tank for Intelligent Design Theory. He now lives in Hopedale, Ohio with his wife, Teresa, and seven children (Jacob, Anna, Faith, Clare, Nathaniel, Beatrice, and Rachel). This is his first book for young people.

Living History Library

The Living History Library is a collection of works for children published by Bethlehem Books, comprising quality reprints of historical fiction and non-fiction, including biography. These books are chosen for their craftsmanship and for the intelligent insight they provide into the present, in light of events and personalities of the past.

TITLES IN THIS SERIES

Archimedes and the Door of Science
by Jeanne Bendick

Augustine Came to Kent
by Barbara Willard

Beorn the Proud
by Madeleine Polland

Beowulf the Warrior
by Ian Serraillier

Enemy Brothers
by Constance Savery

Galen and the Gateway to Medicine
by Jeanne Bendick

God King
by Joanne Williamson

The Hidden Treasure of Glaston
by Eleanore M. Jewett

Hittite Warrior
by Joanne Williamson

If All the Swords in England
by Barbara Willard

Madeleine Takes Command
by Ethel C. Brill

The Mystery of the Periodic Table
by Benjamin D. Wiker

The Reb and the Redcoats
by Constance Savery

Red Hugh, Prince of Donegal
by Robert T. Reilly

The Small War of Sergeant Donkey
by Maureen Daly

Shadow Hawk
by Andre Norton

Son of Charlemagne
by Barbara Willard

The Winged Watchman
by Hilda van Stockum